Past Perceptions

Joy Skye

Published by Joy Skye, 2023.

PAST PERCEPTIONS

First edition. February 9, 2023.

Copyright © 2023 Joy Skye.

ISBN: 979-8215612132

Written by Joy Skye.

This one's for my big sister, Linda.

ONE

'I've lost my muse, Sam. Whatever the hell that was. I stand in my studio, staring at a blank canvas and I feel... nothing.' Monica took another slug of the wine that was fuelling their evening of remorse and regret.

'He said he loved me. But he didn't,' Sam chimed in. 'He was just like the rest of them, looking for his next opportunity.'

Her best friend and agent mimicked her movements, throwing down the last of an impossibly expensive bottle of wine that they had killed within an hour at their regular haunt in Camden. The music was pumping and the creative, successful people around them were doing what they always did on a Friday night. Mingling, making contacts, or, failing that, unfortunate decisions.

'I think you could pay a little more attention to *my* problem,' Monica said truculently, waving vaguely at a passing waiter.

'I think you just need to get laid,' Sam retorted. 'It's not your muse that's blocked. It's your woman's bits. Get some under-the-sheets action and your creative streak will soon start flowing again.'

'And I think you need to stop being such a bitch!' Monica's words hit an unfortunate break in the music and the silence flowed out from their table as everyone in the bar turned to look at them. Sam cocked a lone eyebrow at her, a move she knew he'd spent hours perfecting, and they both burst into laughter.

'Tequila!' Sam shouted gleefully at the tired-looking waiter who'd arrived at their booth in response to Monica's earlier wave.

'Tequila,' Monica echoed in agreement. Some nights called for tequila, and this was definitely one of them. She had an important show scheduled at the end of next month and had nothing to exhibit. Nothing new, anyway. The biggest opportunity she'd ever had, and she was about to blow it, big time. After weeks of worrying about it, she was happy to forget about her problems for a while.

A couple of hours later, they were supporting each other as they staggered down the street towards her flat above the deli on Camden High Street.

'You know what you need? You need a break,' Sam slurred at her as she navigated them around a lamppost and a pile of dog poo.

'A break from you?' she snorted, trying to steer her inebriated agent in the right direction. The fresh night air had gone some way to sobering her up, leaving her in that half world between being the responsible one whilst still feeling slightly fuzzy-headed.

'Nooo. I mean, an actual break. Get away from it all, you know.'

'Not really, Sam,' she said tiredly as she struggled to get her key into the lock. She must get around to changing that bulb. Once they were finally inside her flat, she dumped Sam unceremoniously onto the sofa, where he snorted and mumbled for a moment before starting to snore. She flicked a blanket over him, wondering how he could sleep while making a noise like a foghorn.

Perfect, she thought as she went to the bathroom to wipe away her make-up. There had been enough sleepless nights recently without this new, noisy distraction. She stared at her face in the mirror. She would be thirty-nine next week. Forty wasn't far behind, and the wrinkles were beginning to show. Placing her palms on the sides of her face, she pulled back, admiring the way all the lines disappeared. Maybe she should consider getting some work done? She scoffed at herself in the mirror. *Who for, Monica? Who for?*

The next morning, she awoke to the sound of rain hitting the window and the delectable smell of freshly brewed coffee. She fumbled her way into the threadbare robe that she'd had since she left home and walked through to the brightly lit kitchen.

'Morning, Sunshine,' Sam chirped happily as he expertly flipped a pancake.

'How the hell do you manage to do that?' she asked grumpily as she rummaged in the cupboard for some paracetamol.

'Do what?' he asked, all wide-eyed and innocent, but she could see the knowing glint in his eyes.

'You know damn well what,' she retorted, sinking onto a stool at the breakfast bar. 'Getting completely sloshed, relying on other people to get you home safely, then waking up without a trace of a hangover, as chipper as a chipmunk.'

Sam giggled as he slid a plate of perfect pancakes in front of her, pirouetting to grab the maple syrup that he knew she loved. 'What can I tell you? I've got good genes,' he said happily, sliding onto the seat next to her with his plate. 'Now, about what I was saying last night,' he took a mouthful and groaned orgasmically. 'God, these are good. But, anyway, as I said. I think you need a break.'

Monica paused her chewing of what were infuriatingly good pancakes and gave him her death glare. 'I have neither the time nor the money for a break, as you well know. So please stop bleating on about that ridiculous notion,' she told him firmly. Sam had the habit of getting carried away by ideas, and she wanted to bang the final nail in this particular idea's coffin.

'Ah, there's the thing,' he said, looking pleased with himself. 'I have a, er, friend who's just finished building some villas in France. He's desperate for people to come to stay and review them, practically giving them away, so it won't cost much.'

Monica kept her death glare going, despite the twitch that had developed in her left eye. 'And why should I spend my last few pounds going there?' she asked in her snippiest tone, although her heart fluttered unreasonably at the idea.

'Because, my dear Monica, you need a break. He'll give you a villa for a song, near one of the oldest mediaeval villages on the French Riviera, where you can hang out where the likes of Sartre and Picasso went for inspiration. If you can't reclaim your muse there, then there's no hope for you, and I may as well chuck you off my books and forget your name.'

Monica paused. There was no doubt in her mind that she and Sam would always be friends, no matter what happened with her career, but this idea was beguiling. What she needed was a fresh look on life, something different, and she couldn't remember the last time she'd been on holiday. She found herself nodding as she ate the pancakes. The thought of being somewhere else, somewhere different, was tantalising. She could feel her creative juices firing up as she imagined this mediaeval place with, no doubt, rolling countryside surrounding it. Then the thought of her outstanding bills slammed into her daydream. How could she possibly think about going away when she still had so much to pay out and no obvious way to match it?

'Before you go down that rabbit hole of unpaid bills and whatever,' Sam sniffed at her. 'I've a whole heap of air miles that need to be used, and Gavin, well, let's just say he owes me a favour.'

'I take it Gavin is your "friend" who has built these villas?'

'Yes, he is. Apparently, they are luxury with all sorts of high-end services tagged on. Spa treatments, a top chef providing meals if you want. It sounds fab, to be honest.' Sam looked unusually wistful for a moment before rallying. 'Anyway, it's a done deal. I've booked you in for three weeks starting next Monday.'

'What? I can't go now. Tabatha is due home next week after she finishes her exams!'

'I know. That's why I've booked a flight for her to join you when she's done.'

Monica slumped back on her stool in defeat. Everything Sam had said made perfect sense, and she and her daughter hadn't been on holiday outside of the country, ever. Weekends away at Center Parcs, a trip to the lake district, the odd visit to her parents in Wales when she'd allowed them back into her life. That was the extent of their travels. Surely Tabatha finishing her last year at university deserved something a little more, well, celebratory?

Sam placed a hand on hers. 'Stop worrying, sweetheart. Consider it my birthday present to you. This is exactly what you need.'

TWO

Jacob stared at the email. Somebody he'd met all those years ago on his honeymoon with Sarah had included him in the round robin that was obviously meant to lure people to this new venture. But he had to admit it was tempting. A villa holiday in France? His son, Nate, was being a complete teenage idiot at the moment, getting into trouble at every possible chance, and he didn't know how to deal with him.

He wished to God that Sarah was still here to guide him through these rocky years. He looked around his chaotic office at the college football trophies and awards his team had won since he took over ten years ago. They seemed meaningless right now. It felt like he was losing Nate and he didn't know what to do about it.

'Tell me what I should do, Sarah,' he asked the family picture on his desk. 'What the hell should I do?'

'You need a break, boss,' came the voice of his second in command. 'Season's over. Time to take a time out,' he added, giggling at his own joke as he went through to the changing rooms.

Time out would be great. Actually, it would be fabulous. He hadn't taken a breath since Sarah died. Coping with his loss and being a single dad had taken up every ounce of his time. That and coaching the team had kept him going these last eighteen months. Maybe it was time for a break. He was still staring at the email when he got the call from his buddy at the local police station.

'Hey, Bob. What's up?' he asked without wasting time on niceties.

'Sorry to do this, but we've got Nate. I tried to quieten it down, but Mrs Belswick is pretty determined to press charges this time.'

'Again with the bookshop?' Jacob asked, already pulling on his coat.

'Fraid so, dude. You need to do something with this boy before all hell breaks loose, if you know what I'm saying.'

Jacob knew exactly what Bob was getting at. He and his brother had been up to similar high jinks as kids when Caleb had taken it a step too far, and he'd ignored it. Well, that was a lie. He'd pleaded with his brother to stop, take a different direction. But it had fallen on deaf ears and the end results were available online for anyone to see.

Shaking away that image, he replied to Bob, 'Don't worry. I'm dealing with it.'

He was about to close his laptop when a thought struck him. *Fuck it, a couple of weeks in France will do us both some good,* and pressed the book now button. Once he'd filled in the details, he grabbed his jacket and jumped in his truck, driving the short distance down main street to the police station. He was so pissed with this kid; his blood was thrumming in his veins as he filled out the paperwork.

'Nate,' he grumbled when the boy came shuffling through, clutching his bag of meagre belongings, staring every which way but at him. The boy remained silent until they were in the truck and he hung a left off of main street, and started weaving between the small streets.

'Aren't we going home?' he asked, pulling on his ear nervously.

'Nope. We're going to Aunt Genie's. It's Friday, remember?' Nate just nodded and continued gazing out of the window at the houses sliding by.

'So, what's he done now?' His sister's hard question by way of greeting actually gave him some hope. Stealing books wasn't the worst thing in the world. Not the best thing for sure, but maybe Nate wasn't headed down the same road as Caleb. Maybe he wasn't letting Sarah down entirely. He shrugged as he pulled off his coat, leaning in to kiss her cheek.

'Nothing to worry about, sis,' he said, following her and the tempting smells into the large country-style kitchen where he found his brother-in-law. 'Howdy, John,' he called, stopping to scoop up a crab vol-au-vent and stuffing it into his mouth.

'What's up, bro?' he greeted him cheerily from his seat at the table. With his perennial good nature and even disposition, John was the perfect foil for his more hot-tempered sister. She didn't know how lucky she was.

'Actually, I think I'm going on holiday,' Jacob said, pulling out a chair for himself.

'What's all this?' demanded Nate, who'd slunk in after him and was hovering in the doorway. He looked at his son and smiled.

'I think it's time we both had a break, don't you?' Nate stared at him mutely for a moment. 'I have plans this summer, you know?'

'Well, now your plans include going to France next week,' he answered as evenly as he could, trying to keep his temper in check. There was no way he was going to let the boy rile him into an argument tonight.

'You're going back to France?' his sister asked in surprise, turning from the stovetop. 'Are you sure you're up to that?' The concern on her face made him smile. She'd been his absolute rock after Sarah died, when he had been a complete train wreck, unable to look after himself, let alone his son.

'Yes, I think it's time. Sarah adored France, and so do I. She wouldn't want me to avoid the place just because she's not here anymore.'

Genie gave him a small smile and squeezed his shoulder. 'Good for you. Now get your hulking great form over here and mash these potatoes for me.'

Nate remained quiet throughout the meal, politely responding to questions and passing dishes when asked. But nothing like the vibrant boy who used to hold court at these evenings with his jokes and antics. It tore Jacob's heart to see how much pain he was in; the way Nate had withdrawn so completely into himself that no one could reach him.

'Give it time,' his sister had told him, but he didn't know how long that should be, and was at a loss of how to help his son with his grief.

'So, France, huh?' Jacob said, to break the ice on the ride home. 'Are you excited?'

'You should have asked me,' Nate replied sullenly.

'Is that why you're pissed? Because I didn't ask your permission first? Listen, Nate, the last eighteen months have been hell. The two years before that when your mum was battling that bloody cancer were worse. I just figured we both could use a vacation.'

'Did it ever occur to you that I might not be ready to face it? Going back to the place we only ever went with Mum, only this time...' he trailed off, angrily wiping his nose with the cuff of his jumper. Jacob let out a long breath. Was he that insensitive to his son's needs?

'I'm sorry, Nate. I didn't think. I can cancel if you want? We can go somewhere else, make some new memories.'

Nate chewed his bottom lip, the way he did when he was thinking hard about something. 'Nah. It's ok, I guess.'

'Are you sure?' he asked as they pulled into their driveway. He stopped the truck and turned to his son, adding, 'I think this trip will be beneficial for both of us, just you wait and see.'

THREE

Monica looked out of the window as the short flight from London came to an end. Wonderful sunshine and an azure blue sea so brilliant it took her breath away lay beneath them as the plane banked around and headed for the short runway. She held on tight to the armrests as a jolt of turbulence made the craft shudder before touching down and smiled at the ripple of applause that sounded through the cabin when they stopped.

She still couldn't believe she was here. A couple of days ago, she was in the depths of depression, wondering what the hell she was doing with her life, and now she was in France. She inhaled deeply as they disembarked. There was something exciting about that first waft of warm foreign air that set her pulse racing.

As she waited for her bags, she replaced the bangles that she'd taken off to pass security, then sent a text to Tabatha to let her know she'd landed safely, smiling at the string of emojis that was the reply. Her daughter was over the moon about the trip and couldn't wait to join her in a few days' time.

She spotted one of her bags and pushed through the throng by the conveyor belt, swooping it up just in time. As she waited for the other two bags, she tried to listen to the French being spoken around her. It had been a long time since she'd used her schoolgirl French and she could only understand a word or two of the rapid conversations.

As the crowd thinned, she became nervous, worried that the bags containing her art supplies had been lost, but they finally appeared and with a sigh of relief, she hauled them off and manhandled all of them onto a trolly. They wobbled precariously as she made her way out of the arrivals hall, and she struggled to steer with one hand, the other one trying to keep them in place.

She stopped and scanned the busy concourse; Sam had promised someone would meet her. Spotting a sign held aloft with her name on it, she waved at the man holding it and tried to aim in his direction.

'Here, let me,' he said, striding over and taking the trolly expertly from her. 'Hi, I'm Gavin,' he said, stretching out a hand. She shook it, taking in his tall, well-built frame and model-type looks. With a shock of dark hair and stunning blue eyes, he was definitely Sam's cup of tea, she thought to herself as she thanked him for coming to meet her.

'Not a problem,' he replied. 'I am just happy that a friend of Sam's will be one of my first guests,' he beamed at her. 'How is he?'

There was something in his tone she couldn't quite fathom.

'Oh, you know Sam. Crazy as ever.'

'Yes. He always was a live-wire.'

As they made their way out to where Gavin had parked, he chatted easily, telling her all about the villas and the area, his love and enthusiasm for both shining through as he talked.

'It all sounds absolutely wonderful,' she told him. 'I'm here to paint. I don't know if Sam mentioned that?'

Gavin laughed. 'He mentioned something about finding your muse, so that makes a little more sense now.'

As they left the built-up area around the airport behind, Monica relaxed into her seat, taking in the countryside they passed. It was all so different from her London home, and she could feel the tension draining with each passing mile. Suddenly St Paul de Vence appeared, rising majestically on the cypress-clad hill before them.

'Oh, wow,' she breathed, craning forward to take it all in.

'It always gets people like that,' Gavin smiled at her. 'Although, to be honest, I've been here for fifteen years, and it still does.'

'I'm not surprised,' she said, her eyes roving over the mediaeval village, ensconced safely in its stone ramparts. Gavin guided the car down a narrow lane, heading away from the village.

'We're just down here,' he told her. 'It's possible to walk up to the village. It only takes about twenty minutes, but I offer transfers as well. Here we are.'

As she got out of the car, Monica took in the low level, stone buildings draped in vivid pink bougainvillea set around the pretty courtyard dotted with teeming flowerbeds. There was an ornate stone fountain in one corner, sunlight glinting off of the water, and a large wooden bench under an ancient olive tree in another.

'It was originally an olive press,' Gavin called from the back of the car as he pulled her cases out. 'It's been a devil of a job to renovate, but I love how it's turned out.'

'It looks amazing,' she smiled at him, walking over to help.

'No, no. We'll leave those here; I'll get someone to bring them to your villa. Come on, let me show you around.'

He led her along the path to the villa furthest away and opened the door with a flourish. 'Welcome to Villa Olivier.'

She creased her brow. 'Olive tree?' she asked, walking in and standing in the large, airy living space. Large, modern picture windows that gave a view of the small pool with the valley beyond offset the traditional stone walls and it had that new-build smell of recently dried paint and cut timber.

'Yes, that's right. Not very original,' he shrugged apologetically as he led her through to one of the bedrooms.

'I think it's perfect,' she told him. 'This place is absolutely beautiful, the light in here is fantastic.'

'This is the master bedroom, the other is a twin, both are en suite. I gather your daughter will be joining you?'

'Yes, that's right. She just finished studying literature at Oxford and is looking forward to kicking back and relaxing.'

'I'm sure she must be. Will anyone else be coming?'

'No, it's just us. It's always just us.'

'I'm sorry, I didn't mean to sound like I was prying,' he said, sounding contrite. Monica laughed at his crestfallen face. 'Don't worry about it, Gavin. Tabatha and I are very happy being our own little nuclear family. We've never been anything else.'

'Ok, well let me show you how everything works and then I can leave you to relax.'

Once the tour was complete and her bags delivered, Monica unpacked her clothes, finding homes for them in the spacious wardrobe that ran across one wall. Her room had the same view as the living area, and she kept getting distracted by it. Finally, she gave up trying to be neat, shoving the last of her tops unceremoniously in a heap on a shelf, and hurried to open up her other bags. She grabbed a sketchpad, her pencils, and some pastels and went out onto the terrace, sitting at the table there to work.

It wasn't until her stomach reminded her it was time to eat that she realised how much time had passed. Standing and stretching, she went to raid the welcome hamper. Munching on some Lou Pevre, savouring the contrast between the creamy cheese and the peppercorns that studded it, she poured a glass of chardonnay as she made up a plate of local delicacies and took it back out to the terrace.

Sitting back in the chair as she took her first sip of the crisp, white wine, she exhaled. It was so peaceful here. No road noise, car alarms, or the million other sounds that made up her usual life. Just the distant twitter of birds and nothing else. She gave a silent toast to Sam. It looked like he was right. A bit of peace and quiet was just what she needed.

FOUR

Sitting in the bustling lounge at Heathrow Airport, Jacob and Nate stretched out their legs on their seats, trying to get comfortable on the hard plastic. The early start, the seven-hour flight from Philadelphia, and the fact that the time difference meant it was suddenly tomorrow were all taking their toll.

'Fancy a coffee, son?'

Nate stopped scrolling on his phone and nodded vehemently. 'I think it's essential!'

'Come on, then,' Jacob said, standing and stretching his arms above his head before dropping them, one arm falling easily around the boy's shoulders as they walked towards the Costa Coffee. Jacob ordered a triple espresso in the vague hope it would defeat the jetlag, but Nate went for his regular macchiato. They sat in companionable silence for a while, people watching while they sipped their drinks.

'Didn't you live in London for a while, when you were a kid?'

'Yeah, my dad was stationed over here for work. I must have been...' he sucked in a breath. 'God, I was a bit younger than you when we came back. Twenty-two years ago.' He shook his head at the memory. 'Seems like a lifetime ago.'

'Must have been tough, being dragged around like that. Losing friends.'

'It wasn't great for my social life, no,' he chuckled. 'But it was a good time in my life. I wouldn't change it.'

'Did you ever come back? You know, to visit anyone?'

'I seriously thought about it when I finished college. But the one person I really wanted to see again had never answered any of my letters, so I chickened out.'

'That sucks,' Nate replied succinctly, draining his coffee, then grinning. 'Letters,' he scoffed, waving his phone under Jacob's nose.

'In my day, kids didn't run around with phones in their back pockets! And yes, it did suck at the time. But about a year or so later, I met your mum, so it worked out for the best.'

'I guess so.' Nate glanced up at the boards. 'Look, our gate number's up. We should get moving.'

During the shorter flight to France, Nate nodded off and Jacob thought back to his youth, his time spent in London and the girl he'd had to leave behind. His teenage-self had been outraged at being dragged away. He remembered giving his parents hell for quite a while after they got back to the States. He gave a wry grin. Maybe Nate's behaviour wasn't so unusual.

The grin slipped away as he wondered again why she had never answered. It had torn him apart back then. All of the promises they had fervently made in whispers to each other that last wonderful night, wrapped in each other's arms on her single bed, trying not to make a sound and alert her parents to the fact that he had snuck in through the window.

The captain's announcement that they were landing brought him back to the present. He shook Nate, who woke with a snort, rubbing his eyes.

'We there?' he asked in his usual laconic style.

'We sure are, buddy. You ready to have some fun?'

'Hell yeah,' he replied, unclipping his belt and standing. Pleased to see the boy's enthusiasm, Jacob followed suit, and they pulled down their carry-on's, waiting impatiently in line for the doors to open.

Once they had retrieved their bags and claimed the hire car, Jacob plugged the destination into the navigation system. He sent a quick text to Gavin to confirm they were on the way, then said to Nate, 'Right, the deal is, you can choose the music today. We're gonna take it in turns, OK?'

Another grin appeared on the boy's face. 'You mean I'm going to have to listen to your old fogie music? That's just cruel. I should report you to child services.'

Jacob laughed and cuffed him lightly across the head. 'Stop being a smartass and play something suitable for a road trip!'

The journey took less than half an hour, much to Jacobs' relief. Nate's taste in music mostly veered towards rap, which was just a load of angry people shouting as far as he was concerned, but he let him have his fun, only turning it down for the last couple of miles so he could concentrate on finding the villas.

As they pulled into the driveway and stopped in the courtyard, Gavin came out to greet them.

'Welcome, Jacob,' he said, pumping his hand. 'It's so good to see you again.'

'Great to be here, Gavin. This looks like quite a set-up you've got here.'

'It's not too shabby,' he joked, looking as Nate got out of the car.

'This is my boy, Nate,' Jacob told him. Gavin peered into the car.

'No Sarah?'

There was an awkward silence. 'No, she, er... She passed a while back.'

'Oh my God, I'm so sorry! Christ, I keep putting my foot in it today. Please forgive me.'

'No harm, no foul,' Jacob told him. Even though it had been a sucker punch to his heart, it wasn't this poor guy's fault. 'So, are you going to show us where we are? We're both pretty exhausted and, frankly, I could use a beer.'

'Of course, follow me.'

Gavin led them to the middle of the three villas, giving them the same speech as he had given earlier to his previous arrival about the history of the place. 'Welcome to Villa Lavande.'

'Woah, this is pretty sweet,' Nate said, rushing straight out to look at the pool, leaving Jacob to take the rest of the tour.

'So,' Gavin finished up. 'There's a welcome hamper, and I stocked the fridge with the shopping you ordered.' He opened it as if to prove his words, revealing shelves groaning with produce.

'That's fantastic, thanks. I really didn't fancy having to go on a grocery hunt as soon as we arrived.'

'It's all part of the service,' he grinned with a mock bow. 'Now, if you need anything, you have my number, and you can usually find me in the office block next to the entrance. That's where the staff prepare all of the catering, and we also have a small cinema room if you ever fancy a movie night. The list of treatments and the room service menu are right here.' He picked up a folder off of the kitchen counter and waved it at him.

'Thanks, Gavin. I'm pretty sure we won't need anything today, but I'll check it out.'

Jacob wandered out to the terrace to find Nate, who was snapping pictures of the villa and its surrounding countryside. 'I promised Aunt Genie I'd send lots of shots,' he explained.

'Well done. What do you say we get unpacked and get into that pool?'

'I'm kinda tired, dad,' he groaned, as if he'd suggested a twenty mile yomp.

'We've got to beat the jetlag, Nate. Try and stay up as long as possible, a swim will perk us up.' Seeing his son still didn't look convinced, Jacob winced as he said 'there's a Sonos system, and it's still your turn with the music.'

'Cool!' Nate said and rushed back inside. Following at a more leisurely pace, Jacob went to the fridge and cracked open a beer, taking a long guzzle. He leaned back against the work surface, needing to take a minute. Seeing Gavin had, inevitably, brought back memories of the honeymoon, leaving him emotionally drained. A loud, pulsing beat started up – Nate had obviously worked out the sound system. He came barrelling out of his room in his swim shorts shouting, 'last one in is a pussy!'

Jacob laughed as he watched his son leap up and cannonball into the pool, waves of water splashing up and over the sides. He placed the bottle on the counter and went to get changed, hoping to God the neighbours didn't object to all the noise.

FIVE

Monica had spent the afternoon relaxing in the sun by the pool and imbibing more of that wine than she probably should. *To hell with it*, she thought, *I'm on holiday*. Then she investigated the complimentary products in the bathroom. Stripping off her costume and slipping into a wonderful white Egyptian cotton bathrobe, luxuriating in the feel of it against her bare skin.

She haphazardly slapped on a charcoal facemask and smeared it across her face, then grabbed the hair oil, squirting a dollop onto her head and combing it through her hair, enjoying the coconut aroma. Giggling, she blew a kiss at her reflection before going to the kitchen and cutting cucumber slices for her eyes. Stretching back out on the sunbed, she closed her eyes and placed the slices on them. 'This is the life,' she said to the world in general, and dozed off in the warm afternoon sun.

A shout from next door woke her, followed by a splash, and she became aware of a dreadful booming of music. Lying there for a minute, unable to believe her ears, Monica dithered, unsure what to do. I'll give it some time, she thought. Surely nobody could be that unreasonable. Taking a couple of deep breaths in through her nose, she tried to rediscover the serene composure of before. There was another yell and another, bigger splash, shattering her attempts.

The noise from next door was becoming unbearable. How could she possibly relax with that cacophony going on, she thought angrily? Finally, it became too much to bear, and she stomped out of the front door and along the path to the next villa, hammering on their door for all she was worth. Eventually someone heard her over the music, she caught a snatch of laughter behind the door before it opened, revealing a tall man about her age, in dripping swim shorts, sporting a smile as wide as the Nile.

'What the hell do you think you are doing? This is supposed to be an upmarket resort. People come here to relax, not listen to you blasting out that dreadful music at full volume and disturbing the peace. It really is most inconsiderate of you; I need to find my zen and you are completely ruining everything!'

'Mon, is that you?'

She stopped her tirade and gave a startled look at the man before her. It was the voice that did it. That's what brought the memories flooding back. That and the fact that nobody else, in all her nearly 39 years, had ever been allowed to call her Mon.

'Jacob,' she whispered in shock, staring into those oh so familiar green eyes, her world spinning on its axis as long suppressed emotions washed over her and she sagged against the doorjamb.

'Oh my God, it is you! I can't believe after all this time I'd see you here, of all places.' That familiar grin turned up with its accompanying dimple and her heart lurched, the same way it always had.

With a start, she realised what a fright she must look. Her hair slicked back with nourishing oils, the cucumber slices that had rested on her eyes now clenched in her fist, dripping juices down her. The luxurious white bathrobe that had given her such delight earlier was now speckled with flakes of the dried-up face mask; little black specks having rained down as she had shouted at him.

She'd shouted at Jacob. The only man she had ever loved, and she'd shouted at him, all the while looking like the ghost from Christmas past. *Holy moly, I can not be dealing with this right now*, she thought, gazing at her slippered feet as she rallied for something to say.

'Nobody calls me Mon anymore. And please turn your music down,' she said stiffly, turning and scurrying up the path as quickly as her feet would take her.

Back at the villa, she slammed the door shut and leant against it, her mind racing and her heart pounding. *This can't be happening,* she thought as she hurried into the bathroom to survey the damage.

It was worse than she'd feared. Her sleep in the sun had dried the oil and her hair was sticking up at a weird angle, reminiscent of that Cameron Diaz film she could never remember the name of. The face mask had baked to a light grey, what hadn't flaked off leaving patches across her face, embedded in her wrinkles, making her look like a zombie. Especially now, with her eyes wide and terrified looking. Get a grip, get a grip, she chanted, scrubbing at her face until she'd removed the worst of it, then jumping in the shower to deal with her hair.

She shook the flakes off of the robe, then pulled it back on, rummaging through her handbag to find her phone.

'Sam, it's me,' she hissed when he answered.

'Hello, darling. How is it? Is it wonderful?'

'Yes, it is. Or it was. You will not believe who is staying next door.'

'Ooh, is it someone famous?' he squeaked excitedly. 'Let me guess... Johnny Depp? Brad Pitt? Ooh, I know, Daniel Craig?' He asked hopefully.

'Stop listing the top ten people you'd like to get jiggy with and listen to me. It's Jacob.'

There was a momentary silence, then a hissing of breath. 'Not THE Jacob. The boy who left you and broke your heart?'

'Yes, that bloody Jacob. What am I going to do?'

'Well, there's not much you can do. Maybe this is fate, you know. Like one of those romcoms you like so much bringing the star-crossed lovers back together.'

'We were not star-crossed, he just left me in the lurch.'

'Well, maybe this is your chance to find out what happened. I know he's the reason you've never gotten involved with anyone else.'

'I don't care about all that now. It's really of no consequence, no consequence at all.'

'Methinks the lady doth protest too much. Anyway, where's the harm? Just because he's staying next door doesn't mean you have to talk to him.'

'Sam, I love you, but you can be really dense sometimes. The harm is Tabatha. She arrives in two days.'

'Oh, Christ, of course. That's going to be a bit of a delicate situation.'

'Delicate?' Monica screeched. 'It's going to be a bloody nightmare.'

'Listen, sweetie, relax. Chances are you won't bump into each other.'

'Can't you come and pretend to be my husband?'

A howl of laughter came down the line. 'With the best will in the world, hun, no one is going to believe I am straight.'

Monica sighed. 'I know you're right, but I could use some support.'

'Let me see if I can pop over at the weekend,' he said hesitantly. 'I can't promise anything, though.'

After they said their goodbyes, she ventured back out onto the terrace. It was all quiet now. *At least he had the decency to do something right for once*, she thought crossly, sitting at the table and looking out across the verdant valley. Jacob Riley. After all these years, who would have thought it was possible. She would just have to keep her head down and stay out of his way. How hard could that be?

SIX

'Who was that?' asked Nate, coming in and rubbing himself dry with a pool towel. 'You alright, Dad?'

Jacob shook his head to clear it and smiled at his son. 'I'm fine, it was just the neighbour. We were being a bit noisy, apparently.'

Nate grinned sheepishly, grabbed his phone off of the table, and stopped the music. 'I'm gonna take a quick shower. Are we going to eat something? I'm starved.'

'You are always hungry, Nate. But yes, I'll throw something together.'

He stared after Nate for a minute, still in utter shock. Monica Palmer. What twisted, fucked up fate had brought her here? He traipsed into the kitchen and pulled another bottle of beer from the fridge, staring into space as he flipped off the cap. He heard Nate's shower turn on, which galvanised him into action, opening the fridge again and pulling out the steaks he'd ordered. Working mindlessly, he seasoned them, put a pan on to heat, and checked what salad ingredients they had.

All the while, those intense blue eyes, aflame with anger, flashed before him. He took another slug from the bottle while he waited for the oil to get spitting hot, his mind pulsing with thoughts. He'd known this trip was going to be emotional, revisiting everything that reminded him of Sarah, but he hadn't expected to have to deal with facing his ancient heartache as well. It was too much to deal with.

Throwing some mixed salad leaves into a bowl, he chopped up some vine-ripe cherry tomatoes, then sliced the radishes. Leaving the avocados to add at the last minute, he was whisking up a dressing when Nate came back out. He looked up and smiled at him.

'I'm just going to throw on the steaks, do you want to set the table outside?'

'Sure thing, Dad.'

Nate came into the kitchen and started rummaging through the drawers, peering into the salad bowl as he passed. 'I take it we're still on the healthy eating plan?' he grimaced in distaste.

'Just because football season is over, doesn't mean we can't keep fit!'

'You know I don't really care about that,' he replied, banging the cutlery he'd found on the counter and reaching overhead for some glasses. Jacob took a moment before replying, reaching over his son's head to take out two plates. His desire to impart his love of football on the boy was a constant source of friction between them, and he didn't want to ruin the camaraderie that they'd achieved since the journey began.

'I guess, as we're on vacation, we could let loose a bit,' he said, smiling down at him, hoping for a truce. Nate nodded, his shoulders relaxing.

'That's more like it. We're supposed to be here to enjoy ourselves!'

Nate scooped up the knives and forks in one hand and the glasses in the other before trotting outside. *Fat chance of enjoying myself with all these memories haunting me*, Jacob thought sourly as he flipped the steaks. He finished up the salad, calling to Nate to take it out to the table as he plated the meat.

The sky darkened around them as they ate, the silence only broken by the chinking of their cutlery. All the while, he could feel her presence emanating from next door. He chuckled at the memory of her standing there, looking a complete state, berating him. Monica always was a fiery one. She blamed it on her red hair, but it was one of the things that had attracted him to her in the first place. That refusal to back down from anything or anyone. It had been exciting.

'What are you giggling at?' Nate asked, looking at him curiously over the table.

'I do not giggle!'

'Sure sounded like a giggle to me.'

'I was just expressing my enjoyment of this moment,' he waved his fork vaguely around. 'Being here, with you. Eating good food in a great place.'

'Whatever you say, Dad,' he grinned at him. 'Anyway, what's the plan for tomorrow?'

'Nothing too crazy, I guess. We're still going to be jet lagged, maybe we can check out the village?'

'That did look pretty cool,' Nate agreed, chewing the last mouthful of steak with a groan of content. 'Although not very exciting.'

'It's not supposed to be Disneyland, son. There's a load of info in the villa book about things to do in the area. Why don't you take these in,' he gestured to the empty plates, 'and grab it while you're there?'

Nate grumbled good-naturedly but did as he was asked, returning with it and some more drinks. They sat for another hour, pouring over the villa book, picking out some ideas, until Nate's yawning became excessive.

'I think it's time you went to bed,' he told him, closing the book.

Nate stood and stretched. 'I think you might be right. Are you going?'

'I'm just gonna sit a while longer. Goodnight, Nate.'

'Night, Dad.'

Jacob sat, staring out into the darkness, trying to get his thoughts in order. He was glad that he was here, and even happier that Nate seemed to be coming out of his shell for the first time since his mom had died.

But seeing Monica had thrown up a whole heap of feelings that he thought he'd got over decades ago. All the torment and heartbreak when the silence from over the pond continued, until his younger self finally accepted that she was gone and that she didn't love him, despite the vows they had made.

He had no desire to hash it out with her. What was the point after all this time? No, all he had to do was lie low, and avoid her at all costs until she left. Finally, tiredness overcame him, and he cleared the last of the debris from the table and made his way to bed.

SEVEN

Monica hadn't slept well. The vision of Jacob kept tormenting her. He'd grown into a fine-looking man, still retaining his boyish good looks, but he'd filled out in all the right places and the grey that peppered his dark hair suited him. As dawn broke, she gave up and padded to the kitchen to make some coffee, taking it to the terrace to watch the sunrise.

The colours were outstanding, the pastel hues undulating before her as the sun came up. Unconsciously, she wound her long hair into a bun, sticking a pencil in to secure it, and started sketching. Losing herself in her artistry, thoughts of that horrible time in her life slipped away as she filled sheet after sheet on her pad.

Her phone chimed, distracting her. **Don't forget to eat.** She grinned at the screen. Her daughter knew her too well. Laying down her pencil, she went back inside to see what was left of the hamper. She gazed despondently at the sad contents of the fridge, cursing herself for not being more organised. Remembering the fact that there was room service on offer, she picked up the menu and glanced through all the breakfast options, her stomach rumbling loudly as she read.

Deciding on eggs benedict with a side of hash browns, she called her order through and went to grab a quick shower while she waited. She was pulling on her sweatpants when a rap on the door announced that breakfast had arrived, so she hastily threw on a t-shirt and went to answer it. Gavin was there with a wooden trolly on wheels.

'Good morning, Miss Palmer. I hope you slept well?'

Not wanting to admit that she hadn't, Monica gave him a smile. 'Like a baby.'

'Hopefully one with a decent sleep routine,' he quipped with a grin.

'Thanks for this,' she nodded down at the trolly, the smell rising from the covered dishes making her salivate.

'My pleasure, if you can just sign here?'

She stepped out to sign the paper on the clipboard he was holding and saw Jacob jogging up the drive. Pen in hand, she stood stock-still as she absorbed the sight of him in all his gloriousness. He'd obviously kept up his love of sports. His body was honed to perfection, and even with sweat dripping down his face and staining his shirt, he looked gorgeous. A jolt of desire shot through her, startling her out of her trance, and she scrawled on the proffered form and quickly pulled her breakfast delivery inside.

Appetite diminished by the fluttering butterflies that were now cavorting in her stomach, she forced herself to uncover the plates and take them out to the table. She picked half-heartedly at the food in front of her, trying to make sense of her feelings. She hated Jacob Riley. He'd broken her heart and left her high and dry when she was at her most vulnerable and needed him most. She pushed the plates away angrily. How could she possibly still feel attracted to a man who'd treated her so badly?

Monica heard sounds of chatter and a splash coming from his villa and jumped up. She couldn't stay here. And if he was spending the day enjoying his pool with *whoever*, she thought bitterly, well, she would just go out.

Taking her backpack from the sofa and stuffing some of her art supplies into it, she slipped it onto her back and marched out across the courtyard, bursting into the office.

'Hi, Gavin, you said something about transfers up to the village?'

He looked up from his computer in surprise. 'Yes, yes, I did. Is everything ok, Miss Palmer?'

Realising she might look a little deranged right now, Monica took a breath and smiled at him.

'Call me Monica, please. And everything is perfect,' she lied. 'I'm just feeling incredibly inspired and want to go up to the village to do some sketching.'

He beamed at her words, standing up and taking some keys off of the wooden rack on the wall next to him. 'Well, that sounds like a fine idea, Monica. If you can't find inspiration up there... well, then all is lost!'

His flair for the dramatic, so similar to Sam's, brought a genuine smile to her face, and she wondered again what had happened between these two. They seemed like a perfect match. *So did you and Jacob*, whispered a wicked voice in her head. Pushing those words away with a shake of her head, she followed Gavin out to the car.

He dropped Monica by the entrance of the walled village, handing her a small, folded map from the glove-box. 'Take all the time you need. Just call me when you're done. As you see, it only takes a few minutes to get here.'

'Thanks, Gavin. I really appreciate you being so flexible.'

He waved away her thanks and drove off, leaving her staring up at the ancient walls. *Right, Monica*, she told herself, *let's give your brain something else to think about other than Jacob love 'em and leave 'em Riley.* Shoving the map in her back pocket, she followed the stream of tourists heading up the cobbled walkway and through the arched gateway into the village.

Wandering the maze of narrow streets, all the enchanting little shops crammed into the stone walls soon captivated her. To her delight, there were reams of galleries to browse through, her own need to paint forgotten as she explored them all. Standing in front of a row of three galleries, angling her phone just right and taking a selfie, she sent it to Tabatha with the line, **I think I'm in heaven.**

Tabatha always moaned at her ability to lose hours in galleries, and knowing that picture would make her daughter smile, she continued happily down the street, thoughts of Jacob temporarily forgotten.

EIGHT

Jacob had set an alarm to wake him up at eight local time, to try to get into the groove. He let Nate sleep in, not wanting to disturb him or force him to come on their regular run. Digging his running gear out of a drawer, he dressed and did a few stretches to warm up before heading out. Ignoring the pull from next door, he lowered his sunglasses and jogged out through the gates, impulsively turning left and following the track down through the glade.

It was a beautiful morning, the sun high enough to warm the clear air, and he took in lungfuls of it, marvelling at the contrast of this to his usual route. Westwood was a lovely, small town, but it was still a town. It didn't have any real open spaces, and the rolling vista before him offered a wealth of options for his run. He picked up his pace, determined to keep up his schedule while he was here. *Especially if Nate was intent on them eating off their usual diet*, he thought with a grin.

Trying to discard thoughts of Monica proved pointless, so he let them endlessly swirl through his brain as he pounded out his frustration. Images of her all those years ago, the smattering of freckles that decorated the bridge of her nose, her cheeky smile and the devilish glint in her eyes that had made his teenage blood boil with a desire that had never been matched.

She couldn't be any more different from Sarah if you tried. Their relationship had been quieter, a friendship blossoming into a steadfast love that was set to stand the test of time. Monica had been more like an explosion, demanding his attention when he had arrived at his new school and, within days, captivating him.

His watch beeped to let him know he'd reached the four-mile mark, and he circled around to head back. The uphill incline made the going slower, but he forced himself on, even though he was flagging. Slowing to a walk as he went back in through the gates, he spotted Monica talking to Gavin by her door and immediately started jogging again - there was no way she was going to see him defeated - and he focused on his own door, refusing to even glance in their direction.

'Hi, Dad, thanks for not waking me,' Nate called from the couch as he stumbled in, ready to drop. He leaned over, hands on his knees for support, his breath coming in quick gasps. He tilted his head up to look at him. 'My pleasure,' he wheezed, wiping away the sweat from his brow.

Nate shook his head in disgust. 'I've no idea why you think that running isn't anything but torture.'

'Right now, I may have to agree with you,' he grinned at him. 'Whatcha got there?'

'I was looking through the room service menu. Can we order something?'

Biting back a comment about the healthy granola and skim milk he'd stocked up on, he stood back up and nodded. 'Sure, why don't you go ahead and order something for us while I take a shower and get cleaned up?'

Nate's delighted smile at being in charge of ordering let him know it was the right thing to say. As he showered, his wandering mind drifted next door and idly wondered if Monica was in the shower right now, too. His body's immediate reaction to that illicit thought had him flicking the water onto cold and he stood under the powerful jets until his blood stopped racing.

I have to get her out of my mind; he thought as he furiously towelled himself dry and went into the bedroom to find some clothes. Running a brush through his thick, dark hair, he noted it was time for a cut. It tended towards curly if he didn't keep it short, springing out in an unruly fashion which he hated.

'Dad, you need to sign for this,' Nate called through to him. Tossing the brush aside, he went to see what his son considered luxury breakfast fare.

'Good morning, Gavin,' he greeted him warmly when he reached the door. The unmistakable aroma of bacon and something else, something sweet, hit him and he turned and arched a questioning brow at his son, who just ducked away, a huge grin lighting his features.

'Hi, Jacob. I hope everything has been to your liking so far?' Gavin asked, handing him a clipboard and a pen. 'It's all great,' he confirmed, adding his signature and handing it back. 'How's it all going? Are we the only ones here?'

'No, no. There's a lady next door,' Gavin pointed. 'She's an artist, here to paint.'

So Monica never lost her love of art, he thought, then suddenly asked, 'is she here by herself?'

'Her daughter is joining her tomorrow, but that's it, I believe.'

He pursed his lips and nodded, as if this was of no consequence to him. 'Well, thanks for breakfast. Do we need to bring this back over when we're done?'

'Good grief, no. Housekeeping will clear it when they come in,' Gavin said, looking vaguely scandalised at the suggestion.

Pushing the trolly out to the terrace, he found Nate had set up the table all ready for them. 'Good job,' he praised as he lifted the lid off of the first dish. As he suspected, it contained a mound of bacon. The second revealed a pile of pancakes, oozing in maple syrup, and he started to laugh. 'You don't do things by halves, do you?'

'I ordered fruit as well. You can just nibble on some berries if you'd like,' he told him cheerfully, grabbing the dish of pancakes and loading up his plate. Taking a seat, he took the dish off Nate and followed suit. He looked up and saw Nate's open-mouthed expression. 'When in Rome...' he smirked.

When they finished the feast, Jacob sat back, patting his stomach. He wasn't going to let on to the boy, but he'd thoroughly enjoyed the breakfast. He couldn't remember the last time he'd allowed himself to indulge like this, and it felt good. As they cleared away, he told Nate, 'once we've done this, we'll head out to see St Paul de Vence, OK?'

If Monica was here to paint, she was probably holed up in her villa, so his best bet to avoid her was to get out of the vicinity.

NINE

Monica was sitting at a small courtyard cafe on the edge of the ramparts with a handful of colourful shopping bags at her feet, admiring the view and sipping on some wonderful local wine. She'd had a fabulous morning trawling through the shops after she'd indulgently splurged on some paintings, arranging for them to be shipped to her home.

She was completely relaxed and feeling rather decadent, truth be told, and it had been a while since she'd felt like this. Tabatha had responded to her earlier message with lots of hearts and laughing emojis, and she couldn't wait to see her tomorrow. It had been tough for her, learning that empty nest syndrome was actually a thing when Tabs left home. First for a gap year, backpacking around Asia with her best friend Sally, which was terrifying, and then when she was sucked, quite naturally, into university life. Monica had built a life dedicated to raising a child by herself, and although her daughter had basically been gone for four years, she still hadn't formed a new life just for her. Not really.

Tilting her head back, she closed her eyes, enjoying basking in the healing warmth of the sun overhead. Some sixth sense pricked her skin and her eyes flew open. Coming down the cobbled slope towards the cafe was Jacob. Head and shoulders above the rest of the crowd, he was hard to miss, and her heart quivered at the sight of him. Casting around desperately, hoping for a handy bolt-hole to hide in, she was disappointed. There was nowhere she could run to. She was a sitting duck. She rummaged in the shopping bags, pulling out the scarf she'd bought for her mum and the oversized sunglasses she'd bought as a joke for Tabatha, wrapping the first around her tell-tale hair and slipping the second over her eyes.

Positioning herself deliberately facing out towards the view, she sipped on her wine nonchalantly, hoping to God he wouldn't notice her. Minutes ticked by, but she refused to look, too scared to check if he'd walked on by or not.

'Any reason you're sitting here, wrapped up like Audrey Hepburn in a movie, avoiding eye contact with me?' whispered a familiar voice in her ear. Her heart stuttered at the words, and his breath on her skin made her body ache and her mind freeze, so she defaulted to comedy.

'I have no illusions about my looks. I think my face is funny,' she quoted from her favourite film, watching intently to see if he remembered. The slow grin that stole over his face confirmed he had, and that fact warmed her heart.

'Monica Palmer,' he murmured, causing goosebumps to break out on her skin at an alarming rate. Rubbing her arms, she glared defiantly up at him.

'That's my name, don't wear it out,' she jibed, wishing the ground would open up and swallow her whole. He looked at her with those incredible green eyes with the unique amber flecks, unchanged since she'd last gazed at them so lovingly.

'Can I sit?' he dipped his head at the empty wrought-iron chair opposite her.

'It's a free country.' God, she sounded like a bitch.

He hesitated, then lowered himself onto the chair, which looked ridiculous with his large frame on it.

'Look, Mon,' he began gently, still gazing at her.

'Nobody calls me Mon!'

He sucked in a breath. 'OK, Monica. Seems like we're stuck here, next door to each other, which is probably the last thing you want. But it is what it is. I don't know about you, but I'm just here to spend some quality time with my boy. Nothing else.'

Monica forced herself to keep eye contact, there was no way she was backing down from this. Why would this be the last thing she wanted?

'Ditto,' she replied. 'But with my daughter.'

'Ok, then. Can we agree to let the past be the past and enjoy our vacations?'

'It's called a holiday,' she sniped. 'And yes, I think our ugly past can be most definitely left behind.'

Jacob's brow creased into a frown, but before he could respond, a young man approached, calling out, 'I thought we were going to meet by the gate, Dad?'

He rose in one agile movement, blocking out the sun. 'Sorry, Nate. I bumped into an old friend of mine from London,' he said. 'Come and say hello to *Monica* Palmer.'

The emphasis on her full name had her itching to scratch his eyes out, but she turned towards the boy with her friendliest smile. 'Nice to meet you, Nate. Are you enjoying your visit to France?'

'I hope you're not the fool who never answered his letters?' the boy answered with a grin before carrying on enthusiastically. 'Did you know that James Baldwin lived near here?'

Sucker-punched by the comment of unanswered letters, she still managed to drag up from the recesses of her memory, 'freedom is not something that anybody can be given. Freedom is something people take?'

Nate looked at her in awe. 'Exactly! He was so amazing. I wish I could have met him.'

'Well, Nate, he loved this village. This was where he chose to call home for the last years of his life. Maybe you can soak up some of his spirit while you're here?'

Nodding at her words, he turned to his father. 'Are we going to eat here or back at the villa?'

The chuckle that rumbled out of Jacob and the grin on his face told her this was a familiar story.

'We really should use up some of the food that I ordered. Let's get back,' he said to his son, then turned his gaze back to her. 'Monica, it was wonderful to see you again, especially without that crap all over your face. Enjoy your afternoon.'

She half rose to give him a sarcastic answer, but nothing came to mind and she sank back into her chair, defeated by the emotions washing over her. Jacob Riley was here in France, as cocky as ever, with a son but no wife apparently. Not sure how she felt about that, Monica ordered another glass of wine.

TEN

He was still trembling as he drove them back to the villa. When he'd spotted Monica at that cafe, he'd hesitated, thinking to turn and find another way to where he was meeting Nate. But her desperate attempts at covering up when she'd spotted him had made him laugh. She could always do that. Even when he was really down, Mon had a way that made him forget his woes and laugh at the world, despite the pressures from his parents and teenage angst. It was some kind of bold, long-forgotten teenage memory of bravado that had made him approach the table and whisper in her ear, forcing him to have the conversation he didn't want to start.

'So, who was that?' Nate chattered. 'One of the kids you went to school with?'

'Something like that, son,' he said, glad that the journey was short and he could distract him with the promise of pizza. She looked the same. Exactly the same beautiful, sylph-like girl he'd fallen head over heels with all those years ago. And despite what he'd told her, it was going to be tough to ignore her for the next couple of weeks.

'Pepperoni or Hawaiian?' he asked Nate, as they pulled into the courtyard.

'Pineapple, Pops, every time!' he cried, unbuckling himself and jumping out of the car. Shaking his head at his son's aberrational tastes, he followed him into the villa, taking out the tray before turning the oven on. Monica's words of "our ugly past" came back to haunt him as he pulled the pizzas from their wrappers and placed them onto the tray. Why would she consider their past ugly when she had chosen how it worked out?

'Dad, I don't want to apply for a sports scholarship,' Nate's plaintive voice broke into his thoughts. Jacob slid the pizza-laden tray into the oven and turned to give his son his full attention. 'Ok, so what do you have in mind?' he asked, careful to keep his face impassive. Sarah had always said that their son would be the next Byron, Marlowe or Keats. Never mind there was no money in being a wordsmith these days.

'I actually applied for the International Summer School at Oxford,' Nate admitted. 'And I got in,' he added, a tad more defiantly, staring at him across the breakfast bar.

'Well, that's amazing,' he exclaimed as his heart sank. 'You wanna have a beer? After all, you're only eighteen months off.'

'Nah, I'm good with another Coke,' he replied, sliding his glass along the breakfast bar in the way of all the westerns they'd watched as he grew up. Jacob refilled it without a word and pushed the glass back to him.

'Here's to you,' he said, raising his beer. 'Here's to you, following your heart!'

'Do you mean that? Are you ok with me going away?' Nate's desperate look told him everything he needed to know about the train wreck he'd become since Sarah had died. Jacob took a moment, then smiled at his son, walking around the breakfast bar to embrace him. 'Whatever works for you,' he murmured, patting his back. 'If you're happy, I'm happy.'

He felt bad at the relief he felt when Nate finally went to bed later that evening. He loved the boy beyond measure, but he needed some time alone to digest the emotions thrown up by looking directly at her. The memory of the familiar smell of her skin when he'd leaned in to whisper in her ear, lighting up his insides and setting his pulse thrumming.

Despite his brave words earlier, he wasn't so sure he could forget their past. Not when just seeing her turned back the clock and made him feel like a love-struck teenager again. And then there was the guilt. The guilt that he felt towards Sarah's memory and their life together. Did the fact that he still had feelings for Mon mean that everything that came after her was a lie? Holding up a hand, he counted out the time difference one finger at a time before picking up his phone from the breakfast bar and taking it outside to call his sister.

'Bonjour! How are you, little brother of mine? Is the villa nice? How's Nate? Is he loving it?'

Jacob laughed. 'Woah, one question at a time, sis! In order, I'm fine. The villa is wonderful, you would love it, and Nate, he's doing great. He seems to be coming out of his shell. We actually managed a full-length conversation this evening.'

'Oh, la la, maybe you should extend your trip.' He heard a muted voice in the background, 'John says hi by the way, and bring him back some cheese. But I'd rather you brought me some wine.'

'I'll see what I can do.'

There was a moment's silence, broken when Genie asked, 'so what's up? What's that undercurrent I hear in your voice? Is it bringing up too many memories?'

A yelp of laughter escaped him. 'Good God, Genie, you and all your questions. But as for memories, yeah, you could say something like that.'

'Well?'

'Mon is here. She's staying in the villa next door.'

He heard her suck in a breath. 'Uh, huh. No way, Jacob. you stay away from that girl. I am not watching you go through all that heartache again. No way, no how.'

'She's not a girl anymore, Genie, she must be nearly forty,' he replied, a frown creasing his brow, and he checked the date on his phone as he listened to his sister rant on.

'That makes not a jot of difference. She showed her true colours to you once, don't go looking for a repeat performance,' his sister said so determinedly he had to chuckle.

'Get off your high horse and settle down. It's fine. I had a chat with her today, and we agreed we're just going to enjoy our individual vaca... holidays,' he amended. 'And that's the end of it.'

The snort that came down the line told him his sister didn't believe a word of it. Problem was, he wasn't sure he did either.

ELEVEN

Monica was feeling dizzy as she walked back down the path to meet Gavin, and she wasn't sure if it was because she'd had too much wine, too much sun or too much Jacob, up close and personal. And why had his son said that? About the fool who didn't respond to his letters? Had he lied and painted a different picture to everyone of their breakup?

The whirlpool of thoughts had no ending, and she was feeling nauseous by the time she reached the car. She sank thankfully into the seat with an enormous sigh that had Gavin shooting her a look of concern again as she arranged her shopping bags by her feet.

'How was it? Did you find what you were looking for?'

'Ha. Not really,' she said ambiguously, studiously staring out of the window.

'Well, tomorrow is another day,' he said brightly as he started the car. 'Maybe you'll find more inspiration once your daughter is here.'

Watching the countryside pass by in silence, Monica wondered what these next few weeks would bring. As much as she was desperate to see Tabatha and finally spend some real time with her, she was terrified about what could happen while she was here. She tossed away the idea of just going home as quickly as it arrived. How on earth could she explain that to Tabs? Her daughter knew how excited she was about the whole trip. Going home after a day or two would just look plain weird.

Thanking Gavin when they reached the complex, she double checked with him about the shopping service. She really should get some proper food in now that she had someone else to feed, and told him she'd email the list later.

Back in the villa, she dumped the shopping bags on the counter and fired up the coffee machine, hoping to counteract the wine she had drunk in the village. She needed to clear her head, clear away the tumult of emotions that Jacob had inspired, and settle down to do some painting. That was what she should focus on, not the riddle that was her past.

She had just set up her box easel on the table outside when her phone rang.

'Hi, Gorgeous, how's it going over there? Anything exciting happened?'

'My life is not a soap opera for your viewing pleasure, Sam,' she tutted as she bent to select a canvas from the stack on the floor beside her.

'Well, I have to get my entertainment somewhere!'

'I did have a run-in with Jacob up in the village today,' she admitted, sitting back up.

'Oooh, tell me everything. Was it tense? Were you nervous?'

'You sound like a Panadol advert for headache tablets,' she griped. 'But I guess it was ok. We agreed to basically just keep out of each other's way.'

'That sounds very grown up and very boring. I thought there'd still be unrequited sexual tension between you.'

Jacob's breath on her skin causing goosebumps flickered across her mind and she shivered.

'That's an awfully long silence,' Sam said. 'Does that mean there's still something there between you?'

'I will admit that he is still bloody attractive, but I'm pretty sure he feels nothing for me. That should be obvious by the way he treated me back then.'

'Honey, you don't know what happened. He might have been in a coma for the last twenty years.'

Monica chuckled. 'You really need to stop watching those dramas on Netflix, Sam. Your imagination really doesn't need any help. Anyway, have you thought any more about coming over?'

It was Sam's turn to be quiet. She could hear him huffing and puffing the way he did when he was building up to saying something he didn't want to.

'I thought you were going to give me some support over here. It's your fault I'm in the mess,' she said crossly.

'I don't think you can blame me for the fuck up that was your relationship decades ago,' he snapped indignantly.

'Sorry, Sam, that sounded ungrateful. I'd just like you to be here too at some point.'

'It's just... It's just Gavin, OK. You're not the only one who's had their heart broken before, you know?'

Startled, Monica sat up straighter. Sam was infamous for loving and leaving them. She didn't think he'd ever had anything more serious than a couple of months, max.

'Well, you should have said that before. He asked about you. When I first arrived. In fact, it was one of the first things out of his mouth now that I think about it.'

'Really?'

'Yes, really. Have a think about it, maybe we can both put our past behind us during this holiday.'

She stared out into the distance for a while when the call ended, trying to get back into her creative zone, but it was no good.

Her mind was too unsettled for any chance of her zen returning today. There were too many questions that she needed answers to. She stood and paced the tiled terrace thoughtfully. Maybe she should talk to Jacob again? Despite their agreement, she wasn't sure she was going to be able to ignore him. If she did, she'd just have to try to get him on his own, and make sure that Tabatha wasn't around for that conversation.

Giving up on painting, she went back inside and opened her laptop to make the shopping list for tomorrow, including all of Tabatha's favourite snacks. Once she'd emailed it to Gavin, she realised she still didn't have anything for dinner tonight, so picked up the menu to choose something for dinner. Deciding she deserved a treat with everything that was going on, she ordered the chicken Provençal, dauphinoise potatoes and Tarte Tatin with cream for dessert. A dose of comfort eating and watching a girlie film was in order for tonight. She could worry about what to do about Jacob Riley tomorrow.

TWELVE

'Rise and shine, up and at 'em, Nate, my boy!' Jacob hollered into the darkened bedroom. He heard a groan and the rustling of covers as Nate rolled over. 'Are you awake?' he added.

'God, yes. Stop shouting, will you?' he mumbled. 'What's the emergency?'

'The rental bikes are here. I've got the route mapped out. We need to get breakfast down us and hit the trail.'

'You don't have to sound so damn chirpy about it,' Nate replied. He flicked on the bedside light and looked at him blearily, an enormous yawn erupting.

'Come on, you said you'd give me this. You know how much I'm looking forward to it. I'm just keen to get going.'

When he saw the boy sit up, he went back into the kitchen to finish up making the breakfast. His concession and bribe to Nate was the bacon sandwiches he'd whipped up, a firm favourite since childhood and the only sure way to get him out of bed. He placed the plates on the table, pouring over the map to double check their route for today. The Artists Loop was just around twenty miles long, so not too intensive, and part of it came right past the driveway, making it an obvious choice for their first ride out.

Nate shuffled in a while later, dragging his feet to express his disgust at the whole early morning venture. Jacob couldn't help but smile at his son's disgruntled face.

'So, do you want to tell me more about this summer school?' he asked as Nate dragged out a chair to join him. He glanced up at Jacob warily, his eyes skittering away as he grabbed the coffee pot and poured a cup. 'It's a pretty big deal. There were thousands of applicants from all around the world.'

'That's incredible, Nate. I'm very proud of you,' he said warmly. 'I just wish you'd mentioned it before.'

'I didn't think I'd get in, and if I did, I didn't think you'd let me go.' Nate finally looked directly at him, his eyes shining with emotion and a flicker of a challenge.

'Well, you did get in, and as I said yesterday, I'm open to the idea. Give me some details.'

He watched in amazement as Nate lit up like a firework while he expounded the wonders of Oxford, the history, the courses, and the libraries. He barely touched his breakfast as the words tumbled out of his mouth, as if they'd been suppressed for a long time and now couldn't be contained. When he ran out of steam, he remembered his sandwich and took a huge bite, eyes still sparkling with excitement.

'Well, I'm sold,' Jacob told him, draining the last of his orange juice. 'How much is this gonna cost me?'

Nate blew out a breath through his nose. 'I was thinking you could let me have early access to my trust fund? I want to pay for this myself.'

Jacob frowned. He and Sarah had set that up specifically for his education, to give Nate choices. But not until he was twenty-one.

'Come off it, Dad,' he cried, seeing his hesitation. 'You offered me a beer yesterday because I'm nearly of age, yet you won't let me have this for my education? That's insane, and you know damn well Mum would have let me.'

Stung by the truth of everything he'd just said, Jacob stood, picking up his plate as he fumbled for a reply. 'You're absolutely right,' he admitted. 'About all of that. When does it start?' he asked with a smile to show his wholehearted support, and turned towards the kitchen.

'In two weeks,' Nate replied quietly. 'I know that cuts into our time here, but I figured I could go straight from here to England. It's easier.'

Jacob's steps only faltered for a beat before he closed the distance to the sink to rinse his plate. It seemed like his son had everything figured out, and as much as it killed him to admit it, he couldn't find a single flaw in the plan. It wasn't like he wanted to go off backpacking in some dangerous country with his mates. There was no reasonable excuse he could give not to allow this to happen. Especially the one where he didn't know what he would do without Nate to look after for two months.

When he turned back to the table, he had his best supportive smile plastered on his face. 'Well, that all sounds great. We can hash out the details later. But now I think we should hit the road.'

Nate's whole body sagged in relief, and he grinned back at him. 'Ok, just give me five minutes to get ready.'

He leapt up and bounded back into his bedroom, and as Jacob stared after him, he tried to balance the opposing emotions that were punching him. On the one hand, he was delighted that Nate had found something he felt so passionate about that he was prepared to stand up for himself. On the other, it meant that he had to let go of what had been his only reason for getting out of bed some days in the past months. Knowing Nate needed him had been the driving force that had got him through his grief, and he wondered vaguely what the hell he was going to do without him.

Shaking off his concerns, he cleared the table and packed a bag with supplies for their day out. By the time he was organised, Nate was ready, and they wheeled the bikes across the cobbles to the gateway before mounting. Taking it easy at first to warm up, they cycled up the hill towards St Paul de Vence, having to work harder as they left the village behind and the terrain became steeper. Their idle conversation petered out as breathing became more urgent, and when they reached Baou de la Gaude, they both slipped off of their bikes, thankful for a break.

Proffering Nate a water bottle, they both stared out as they drank thirstily, taking in the incredible vista splayed before them. It felt like they were on top of the world and could see right across the valley to the coastline of the Côte d'Azur, and the emerald-coloured waters of the Mediterranean Sea beyond.

'Wow,' Nate said, wiping away a dribble of water from his chin.

Jacob spluttered out a mouthful. 'I hope this summer school teaches you to use bigger words than that, and preferably more than one at a time.'

Nate punched him playfully on the shoulder. 'Come on, old man, let's see if you can make it the rest of the way around without passing out!'

They continued on up to Saint Jeannet, both grateful when the road took a downward turn as they hit the home stretch through Vence and then back to the villas. They were laughing and joking as they pushed the bikes back through the gateway, standing to one side as Gavin's car swept through.

Walking towards his villa, Jacob halted, suddenly aware that Nate wasn't contributing to their discussion about dinner anymore. He turned back and saw the boy had stopped and was gawking at the young woman that was getting out of the car. She was tall, even in the flat sandals she donned. The bold, floral print sundress skimming her thighs, the colourful bangles dancing down her arm and the overlarge sunhat and sunglasses combo she wore with confidence let him know immediately that she was Monica's daughter. There was something so familiar about her she couldn't be anyone else.

He watched as she gracefully looked across her shoulder, sensing Nate's gaze, lifting her sunglasses to return his appraisal with a look that Jacob couldn't see from where he was standing. Whatever had been in her eyes had the boy scrambling into action and trotting towards him without a backwards glance. A flicker of apprehension shot through him at Nate's reaction. Looked like he had a second reason for avoiding the guests next door now.

THIRTEEN

An insistent rapping on the villa's front door brought Monica back to reality with a thud. She'd woken up this morning, her head filled with half-remembered dreams, and immediately started to paint. Glancing around, she could see the sun had crossed over her head whilst she was lost in her world and it was now late afternoon. Wiping her face distractedly with the back of hand, smearing a smudge of blue across her brow, she padded inside to see what the ruckus was about.

'Mum,' cried Tabatha, engulfing her in an enormous hug, squashing the breath out of her. Returning the fervent embrace, she laughed. 'I'd totally lost track of things. Hello, my darling girl.'

Tabatha stood back, gazing at her with an amused look as she recognised the artistic-fuelled glaze to her mother's eyes. 'Have you eaten today? Drunk any water? Been for a pee?'

Monica waved vaguely at the interior of the villa. 'I'm sure I must have been to the bathroom at one point.'

'Hmm, come on. Let's get inside and get you sorted. I'm dying to see the place.' Tabatha pushed her unceremoniously backwards and into the living area. Monica rallied her brain while Tabatha ran around squealing with delight at every new find.

'This place is amazing,' she exclaimed, running back in. She threw her hat on the sofa, then twirled around with her arms stretched out, her dark curls bouncing joyously in agreement before plopping down next to her hat. 'We're going to have such fun.'

There was another knock on the door. 'Oh, that'll be Gavin. He said he'd bring my bags and the shopping that you ordered.' She leapt back up and raced to answer it. Smiling at her daughter's boundless energy, Monica followed and together they carried everything in, taking the shopping bags into the kitchen.

They worked in familial harmony, unpacking all of the food Monica had ordered, quickly running out of space.

'Good grief, Mother, are you planning on feeding the five thousand?' Tabs grinned at her from her crouched position, as she shoved some things aside in the fridge to make room for the next batch. That done, she stood and stretched, pulling a hair band off of her wrist and catching her errant hair up in a ponytail. 'Shall we make up a plate of goodies? I'm starved.'

'It's starving, dear, and that's why I ordered so much. Your appetite never ceases to amaze me,' Monica replied, grabbing a platter from the shelf and placing it on the counter. 'Pick out some cheese, and I'll wash the grapes.'

They chatted happily as they gathered a snack together. 'How did your exams go?' she asked her, taking some sliced ham out and putting it on a separate plate.

'Bloody exhausting,' came the emphatic reply. 'That's why I was so thrilled that Uncle Sam organised this for us. It's perfect timing. I plan to lie on that sunbed out there and read for as long as possible.'

'We'll see how long that lasts,' Monica replied darkly, knowing all too well her daughter's inability to sit still for more than five minutes. Picking up the food-laden plates, she nodded at the fridge. 'Grab the chardonnay and a couple of glasses, will you? The opener is in that drawer next to the hob.'

Outside, Monica was just moving her artwork to make space for their feast when Tabatha came out.

'Wow, look at these,' she said, putting down the wine and glasses and coming over to look. She walked along slowly, taking in all four paintings. 'These are a bit different,' she glanced at her mum. 'More... I guess they're more emotional? I love the colours.'

'I was just playing around,' Monica said dismissively. 'Let's lean them against that wall to finish drying.'

As they sat and enjoyed their meal, her gaze kept being drawn to the paintings. The bold use of colour was a new direction for her, as she was famous for her use of pastels. But it wasn't this fact that kept her eyes darting back to the canvases. It was the fact that, now she could appreciate them with a detached eye, removed from her creative flurry of this morning, she could see exactly what she had painted. They were snapshots of her relationship with Jacob. Moments in time that she'd believed she had long since forgotten.

The picnic, laid out on a brightly coloured blanket on a sunny beach, was the day trip to Brighton they had stolen, bunking off school to laze in the sun and splash in the sea. The Thames lit up at night brought back memories of riding the London Eye, kissing all the way around, completely ignoring the view and the disapproval of the older group of ladies in their carriage. A raft of penguins, swimming effortlessly underwater, was from one of their many trips to the zoo.

And the final one depicted a faceless couple in a narrow bed, wrapped in each other's arms, clinging to each other in desperation and swearing their undying love for each other. That had been their last night together. When he had snuck into her bedroom and she had finally given herself to him completely, so certain was she that this was forever.

'Mum. Mum!' Tabatha's insistent voice snapped her back to the present.

'Sorry, I was miles away.'

'I could see that. What's up, don't you like your work?' she asked, nodding in the direction of the canvases. 'I really like them,' she went on, snatching up another hunk of Camembert and chewing thoughtfully as she looked at them.

'I'm not sure. I'm not sure if it's the right direction for me to go.' Monica told her, trying to deny to herself that it was some of the best work she'd ever done.

'That's crazy, they're amazing. You've always told me to follow my heart and my dreams. Something here has obviously fired your imagination,' her arms waved around expansively as she spoke, her bangles jingling down her arms. 'Go with the flow. Isn't that what you taught me?'

Monica knew exactly what had fired her imagination and it wasn't the rolling hills or mediaeval villages of France. It was seeing Jacob again, stirring up all these memories, and she didn't know if she had the courage to face more of her past let alone commit it all to canvas.

FOURTEEN

Nate was delighted to find a note from his dad the next morning, letting him know he'd gone out for a run. Relieved that he had been spared that torture, he grabbed some breakfast and settled on the couch to finish reading his book. That's where Jacob found him when he came staggering back in, his face almost fuchsia, hair stuck to his head in sweaty lumps.

Nate looked at him in distaste over his book. 'So that was fun, huh?' he quipped, laying the book on the seat next to him.

Jacob gave him a hard look while catching his breath. 'Not all of us are sloths,' he said as he went to get some water.

'I have been exercising my mind, thank you very much.'

'That's something, at least,' he conceded. 'I'm going to have a shower, then we can work out what we're going to do today.'

Nate shook his head in despair. 'Can't we just hang out here? Why do you always have to be running around? You should learn to chill out.'

'Hey, what can I tell you? It's just the way I am, but you can pick something today, ok?'

Nate gave an exaggerated sigh as he stood up. 'I'm just going to pop over to the office. Apparently, there's a lending library over there. I want to see if they have anything interesting.'

Jacob snorted. 'So, the extra I paid for the weight of all those books in your luggage...?'

Nate just grinned and waved off his comment as he walked towards the door. When he pushed open the door to the office, Gavin looked up from his computer screen and smiled.

'Good morning, Nate. How are you today?'

'Morning, Gavin. I'm great, thanks. I've just come to check out your lending library?'

'Oh, that's just behind you. On the shelves next to the window over there.'

Nate eyed up the contents of the bookshelves, looking for something he hadn't already read. He was reading the blurb on the back of an interesting-looking biography when he saw her. That girl from yesterday, walking towards the office. He gulped and dashed a hand through his unbrushed hair, painfully aware that he was still in the sweatpants and t-shirt he'd slept in.

He listened in as she chatted with Gavin, discussing the best beaches along the coast and arranging for a taxi. He loved her accent; he could listen to her talk all day. As she turned to leave, she spotted him and the books and came over.

'Find anything interesting?' she asked with a quirk of her lips that he couldn't stop staring at.

'Umm...' he grabbed a random book and held it up.

'Theroux? Good choice. He's a bit of a dick, but his descriptions of Asia back in the 70s are fascinating.'

She gave another quick, brilliant smile and turned away. Nate stood rooted to the spot as he watched her stride back to her villa, her beautiful hair bouncing with every step. He slapped his forehead with the book. His first chance to impress her and all he had managed was *Umm?*

Jacob looked up from his iPad when Nate came back in, clutching two books to his chest, looking downcast.

'What's up, buddy? Not enough choice?'

'I found a couple that could be good,' he said, putting them on the table. 'Dad, can we go to the beach today?'

'I guess,' he replied, not overly enamoured with the idea. 'Where did you have in mind?'

'I read Antibes is a great spot,' he said, ducking his head, his eyes focused on the books on the table.

Jacob's face creased into a bemused grin at his son's weird behaviour, but played along. At least it got them away from the villas and away from Monica and her daughter.

'Sure, why not?'

While Nate went to get ready, he looked up Antibes to see if he could figure out what the attraction was. The beaches looked spectacular and the Old Town might be worth a visit. *Maybe it won't be so bad after all*, he thought as he put his iPad away.

It was just a half hour drive and then they were strolling along the seafront, beach bags hitched on their shoulders, looking for a good place to settle. They managed to find a couple of free sunbeds on the waterfront and staked their claim by laying out their towels before stripping down to their swimwear. Jacob cast around, looking at the cafes and restaurants that lined the road behind them.

'Look,' he nudged Nate and pointed. 'That one has your name all over it.'

Nate glanced over and saw his dad was pointing at a place called Maison de Bâcon, and even with his limited French, he got the gist. 'Sounds like heaven,' he grinned. 'Come on, let's test out the temperature of the water,' and he raced into the waves. Jacob quickly followed, sinking back into the warm water with a sigh.

He hadn't swum in the ocean since the last time he and Sarah had been away, and he'd forgotten how wonderful it felt to just float along, allowing the waves to take you this way and that with no purpose or direction, just enjoying the moment. A remarkable sense of peace washed over him as he relaxed, the perpetual stress of the last few years ebbing away with each swell and dip of the water. He hadn't realised how tightly wound he'd been until now. Its absence left him limp with relief as he settled onto his sunbed.

He glanced at Nate, who was pulling the inevitable book out of his bag, no doubt getting ready to spend the whole day engrossed in its pages.

'Good call, Nate,' he said to the boy, as he slipped on his sunglasses and rested his head back. This was just what he needed. A perfect, relaxing day.

FIFTEEN

'Ha! I knew it,' Monica crowed when Tabatha came back and told her about the planned excursion. 'Less than twenty-four hours and you already have itchy feet.'

Not bothering to deny it, Tabatha just smiled. 'I want to take you for a day out, beach, shopping, lunch. My treat.'

'I thought all students were poor?' she asked with a grin, before draining her coffee.

'Grandma sent me some money. My reward for making it through university, so I thought we should spoil ourselves.'

'Oh, darling. That's very sweet, but that money is meant for you. For all of your hard work.' *Guilt money*, she thought angrily.

Tabatha drew herself up to her full height, a huffy look on her face. 'Mum, if it wasn't for you, I wouldn't have been there in the first place. I know all of the things you have done without over the years to pay for everything.'

'It was hardly a sacrifice,' she replied lightly, walking past Tabatha as she took her cup to the sink.

'For goodness' sake, let me do this for you. Why won't you accept the fact that I appreciate you and want to do something nice?'

She rinsed her cup and placed it in the dishwasher before responding. 'Well, there is a gallery I wanted to go to in the Old Town there.'

'There you are. We'll get the taxi to take us there first, and then go somewhere nice for lunch,' Tabatha said triumphantly.

'OK. And thank you,' she said, pulling her in for a hug. 'But none of that vegetarian nonsense. I want some proper food!'

Laughing at her, Tabatha pulled away. 'I'm sure we can find somewhere we'll both enjoy. Go on, scoot. Get your beach things together. The taxi will be here soon.'

They were in the taxi, discussing the things they wanted to see in Antibes, when Tabatha suddenly asked, 'do you know anything about the people staying in the villa next door?'

Monica's heart stuttered. Debating the best way to respond, she hesitated. Should she admit to knowing them or would that just lead to more questions? Tabatha carried on before she could decide. 'I bumped into the boy in the office. He seemed sweet.'

Just like his father, she thought and muttered, 'appearances can be deceiving.'

Her daughter looked at her askance, her brows drawn together.

'Just some American guy with his son as far as I can gather,' she blurted. 'Oh look, I can see the walls of the town.'

They went to the Picasso museum first, taking the time to appreciate the view from the castle's rocky outlook, as well as the works of art that were on show. When Tabatha got bored with looking at paintings, they spent some time exploring the narrow, pedestrian streets bursting with old-fashioned shop-fronts flaunting their wares.

'You don't have to buy all of your gifts today. We are here for another couple of weeks,' she told her daughter, when she bounded out of yet another shop clutching a rainbow of gift bags in one hand.

'Leave me alone. I'm enjoying myself! I've been living on a tight budget for so long that this makes a delightful change.'

'Fair enough. But I, for one, need a coffee, or something stronger, before we do anything else.'

They found a quaint cafe overlooking the ocean and sat at a table in the shade of a large blue and white striped umbrella. Monica ordered their wine while Tabatha checked her phone to find somewhere suitable for lunch. When the waiter arrived with their drinks, she put her phone down and took her first sip with an appreciative sigh.

'So, have you thought about what you want to do for your birthday?'

'This entire trip is my birthday treat,' Monica replied. 'That's more than enough.'

'Oh, Mum,' she said, exasperated. 'Trust you to be so blooming reticent. We have to do something to celebrate.'

'I don't *have* to do anything. It's my day after all.' Seeing her daughter's crestfallen face, she thought for a moment. 'But I'll think about it. Maybe we can have some spa treatments at the villa?'

Not looking entirely convinced, Tabatha took another sip of wine. 'After we finish these, let's go for lunch. I'm famished.'

Monica beamed at her, happy they'd shelved the birthday discussion. She wasn't ready to accept that she was nearly forty, not by a long shot. She'd be quite happy if they just ignored the day entirely, but she had a feeling she wasn't going to be allowed to. They got a taxi for the short ride to the place Tabatha had chosen from the restaurants that lined the shore.

'It's right next to a great stretch of beach,' she told her excitedly. 'I'm looking forward to going for a swim in the sea.'

'It will make a nice change to swim in warm water,' Monica agreed as they pulled up. The only time they'd swum in the sea together had been in the Irish Sea when they occasionally visited her parents in Wales, which could best be described as bracing.

As they waited to be seated, Monica looked around the chic restaurant appreciatively. High-beamed ceilings and muted tones made the large space look inviting, and the terrace that fronted the sea looked like the ideal spot to enjoy their lunch. The waitress picked up two menus from the podium by the door, asking if they would like to be seated outside on the terrace. Monica confirmed they would, and the young woman led them out, pointing to the last free table at the end.

As they followed her along past the other diners, she covertly looked at their plates, trying to see what looked appetising. She ground to a halt when her eyes locked with Jacob's startled green ones. Tabatha bumped into the back of her and she stumbled forward a step, her hand shooting out to catch her balance on the table. His face creased into a wry grin.

'Of all the gin joints in all the towns in all the world...' he said, in a dreadful parody.

'Your Bogart hasn't improved, then?' she asked swiftly, glancing to where their waitress was waiting for them by their table. There was an embarrassed silence as they stared at each other.

'Aren't you going to introduce us, Mum?' Tabatha demanded over her shoulder. Unease shooting through her, she glanced at Tabatha, happy to note she still had her sunglasses on. Monica took a deep breath and returned her gaze to the two expectant faces.

'Jacob, Nate, I'd like you to meet my daughter, Tabatha.'

SIXTEEN

Jacob had no idea why he'd parroted those words, a deep memory of their youthful game, once they'd discovered their mutual love for black and white movies. Despite what both of their parent's thought was going on, they spent most of their time watching films.

But with three sets of eyes on him, he didn't have time to process that, so he rose awkwardly into a half crouch over the table and stretched out his hand.

'Jacob Riley, pleased to meet you.' The young woman reached around her mother to receive his grasp, both of them pausing on contact as something slithered between them. The girl seemed to be stuck for a response, so Jacob carried on. 'And this is my son, Nate.' He pulled his hand from her grasp and ruffled the boy's head, seemingly annoying both kids at once. Nate scowled at him briefly before turning to Tabatha.

'We already met, Dad. Hi, how you doing?' he asked her breathlessly.

Jacob chuckled to himself. The boy was obviously smitten.

'How are you finding Theroux?' she asked cooly, although where she was looking was a damn mystery with those ridiculous glasses she had on.

Nate half tugged a book from his bag. 'Just started it. I'm enjoying it so far.'

'So, Tabatha. It's great that you could join your mother on holiday.... in between?' Jacob interjected, desperate to end this awkward situation and remove Monica from his immediate sight.

'I've just finished uni,' she responded happily, a wide smile on her face. He could see Mon in that smile and the freckles across her nose, but that was about it. She was much taller and her dark hair was nothing like her mother's.

'So that would make you, what, twenty-one?' Jacob asked, silently doing the maths. Monica hadn't waited too long after he left, it would seem.

Tabatha opened her mouth to reply, but Monica butted in. 'It's rude to ask a lady her age,' she said primly. 'Come on Tabs, that poor waitress is waiting for us.'

Both of them swivelled to watch the two women walk along the path to the table at the end where they graciously took their seats. Jacob turned away, glad his back was to them.

'So, Nate. Shall do what we said and skip dessert, get an ice cream later?' he asked, continuing the discussion they'd been having before they were interrupted. His heart was still pounding from the encounter and he wanted to leave. But Nate was gazing beyond him to where Tabatha was sitting.

'I could eat dessert,' he said, glancing hopefully at Jacob. Resisting the urge to tease the boy, he nodded and passed him the menu. He, of all people, knew what it was like to be infatuated by a member of the Palmer family. The memory of the first time Monica spoke to him was still etched in his brain. His tongue-tied responses to her barrage of questions about his arrival at her school still made him blush to this day. It had been mortifying. His teenage-self had avoided her for days after that, terrified she would make him look foolish again.

The millefeuille that Nate ordered looked amazing, but was completely wasted on the boy. Jacob was sure he didn't taste a thing as he robotically scooped up spoonful after spoonful, eyes still laser-focussed elsewhere. When they'd finished, Jacob paid the bill, and as they stood to leave, he glanced back at Monica. She was laughing at something her daughter had said, looking completely unconcerned by his presence and absolutely beautiful.

Ignoring his body's reaction to her, he walked out of the restaurant with a grim look of determination on his face. There was no way he was going to let himself fall under her spell again.

Back on the beach, Nate flopped straight back down onto his sunbed with his book, but Jacob couldn't settle. He felt ansty and needed to do something. Stripping off his cargo shorts and t-shirt, he dived back into the water and set a goal to swim out to a distant, fluorescent orange buoy. Pounding through the waves with a steady front crawl did nothing to dispel the images of her, though. It was infuriating. He picked up his pace, soon reaching his goal. He doggy paddled for a moment, debating if he should go further. But common sense kicked in and he turned and headed back to the shore at a more leisurely pace, his body groaning at the abuse of the unfamiliar workout.

Nate barely acknowledged his presence when he returned, completely absorbed in his book. He dried off and lay on his sunbed. After a few minutes, he reached into his bag and pulled out his AirPods. Popping them in his ears, he selected a playlist from his phone and closed his eyes, resolved to try to relax again. He must have drifted off, as when he came to, Nate was no longer next to him and he felt sunburnt. Looking out at the water, he saw his son a few feet out, floating on his back in the shallows, and stood to go and join him.

But his eyes were drawn to the sight of Monica and her daughter, walking down the beach looking for empty sunbeds. It was late afternoon, so the place was packed out, and it took just seconds for him to work out that the only beds available were just a couple of spaces up from him.

'Nate!' he called quickly, walking towards the sea. 'Nate!' His son heard him and manoeuvred into a standing position.

'Come on, son. It's time to go.'

'Aw, dad. Why?'

'Because I said so, that's why,' he said, more sharply than he'd intended. Nate waded ashore, grumbling under his breath, but obediently packing up his things.

'You really need to learn how to chill the hell out,' Nate told him as they walked back to the car. 'We're supposed to be on vacation, which means put our feet up, hang loose. Not run around like headless chickens.'

The boy was absolutely right of course. He had no defence against his actions. Well, none that he could explain to his son. But the problem was, despite his best efforts, he was finding it harder and harder to ignore the proximity of Monica Palmer.

SEVENTEEN

Monica was so unsettled at bumping into Jacob, she barely touched the beautifully presented wood-fired sea bass that she had ordered. What were the bloody odds? The whole of the Côte d'Azur to choose from and they'd both ended up in the same place. Tabatha peppering her with questions about them didn't help matters.

'So, you know that guy?' she asked as soon as they took their seats.

'Oh, vaguely,' she answered airily. 'Is there anything on this menu you can eat?' she queried, flicking through the pages.

'Yes there is, I checked. Stop deflecting,' Tabatha replied, pushing her sunglasses up onto her head and giving her a beady look. Staring back at those eyes that were so similar to her father's, she could see that her daughter would not let this go.

'So why didn't you tell me when I asked about them?' She demanded, as Monica brainstormed the best way to deal with the situation.

'I didn't think it was of any consequence,' she said eventually. Monica took a sip of wine to give herself a moment. 'Jacob is just someone who was at my school for a couple of years. I don't really remember him that well, truth be told.' Fingers firmly crossed under the table and out of sight, she hoped to God that Tabatha would believe this blatant lie and let this go.

'Well, I think it's great. Nate seems nice. Maybe we could all hang out?'

Sucking through her teeth, Monica laughed inwardly and the farcical position she was in. This was becoming a nightmare. What was supposed to be a relaxing, girlie chill-out holiday was turning into a complicated travesty of Shakespearean proportions.

'We'll see,' she said, in the way of mother's everywhere who had no intention of doing the thing that their children were requesting. Tabatha's face screwed up, perplexed, but the waitress arrived to take their orders and distracted her.

The conversation drifted elsewhere as they were served their food, Tabatha regaling her with stories from the last term at university and her hopeful plans for the future, all the while expressing her rapture over her artichoke and truffle risotto. Luckily, her constant chatter didn't require too much input from Monica, and she kept what she hoped was an attentive look on her face as her thoughts wandered off to the man who had broken her heart so completely all those years ago.

Fate obviously had a twisted sense of humour, sticking him next door and in a situation where they couldn't avoid each other, it would seem. She debated again about having it out with him, but did she really need to hear him say he hadn't loved her at all? That leaving for America had been a godsend to get him away from her and it hadn't come soon enough?

She shook her head to clear those thoughts and the pain they dredged up. There was no point going over old ground and opening those wounds that she'd spent years trying to heal. With a start, she realised Tabatha was staring at her expectantly.

'Sorry, what did you say?'

'I said, shall we go to the beach now? Are you alright?' she asked, concern filling her eyes.

'Yes, yes. I'm fine. I was just thinking about a painting I want to do.'

'Do you need us to go back so you can start on it?' Tabatha asked. Smiling at her daughter's deep understanding of her artistic process, she shook her head.

'Not right away. It's just something I'm mulling over. Let's go to the beach. I could do with some sun.'

She saw him. She saw him leap like a scalded cat, grab his son and hightail it away as if the devil were at his heels. *Maybe his guilty conscience is bothering him*, she thought as they settled on the sunbeds, surprised how bothered she was by his actions. *This sucks*, she thought, slapping spf 100 on to protect her fair skin from the brilliant sun, then adjusting her sun hat as she lay back. *Over twenty-two years of trying to get over the guy and all he has to do is show up and I'm a hot mess again.*

'Did you say something?' Tabatha asked, looking down at her as she got ready to go for a swim.

'No, sweetie, nothing important.'

'Are you coming in?'

'Not yet. I'll let my sunscreen soak in. You know how careful I have to be.'

She watched as her daughter pulled her hair back into a ponytail and strode down to the shore with those impossibly long legs of hers. She could see a couple of young guys a few beds along, gawping at her as she waded in a few paces, then dived forward in one graceful movement. Oh, to be that young and beautiful again, she thought wistfully. With the world at your feet, and all your options ahead of you, just waiting for you to choose.

She'd had all that once. Perfect school reports, a perfect boyfriend. Her future so bright and shiny it was blinding. But one night of ill-conceived passion had changed all that, altering the trajectory of her life in one fell swoop. Not that she regretted having Tabatha. She wouldn't change that for all the money in the world, she loved her daughter fiercely.

But sometimes she couldn't help but wonder what might have been if things had worked out differently. If she'd never met Jacob, and had gone on to have a career so much earlier in life rather than waiting until her baby grew up. Or, better still, if he'd answered her damn letters and come flying back to rescue her and they'd had the life they had planned.

She jumped up, shedding her hat and her shades, and ran towards the water. To hell with the sunscreen and to hell with Jacob. She was sick of being governed by things she had no control over, and enjoying this holiday was her number one priority from now on.

EIGHTEEN

When Jacob came back from his run the next day, it startled him to find Nate and Tabatha out on the terrace, zealously debating their favourite literature.

'Oh, hi dad,' he said a little sheepishly. 'Tabs came over to lend me a book. That's alright, isn't it?'

'I guess so,' he replied, staring at the girl. There was something disconcerting about her that he couldn't put his finger on. He checked the time on his watch. 'I'm going to have a shower, then we can decide about lunch,' he told him, hoping she would take the hint and leave them be.

But when he came back out, she was still there. In fact, she and Nate were in the kitchen preparing food.

'What's all this?' he asked, his heart sinking.

'I invited her to join us for lunch. We're making something from the leftovers.' Nate had such a pleading look on his face he couldn't deny him.

'What about your mum, Tabatha? Won't she be wondering where you are?'

Tabatha glanced up from the tomatoes she was cutting and gave a shrug. 'She's painting. She probably won't even notice I'm not there.' There was no accusation in the statement, just a comment on how things were. He watched her for a moment, noting that she quartered then sliced the tomatoes the same way that he did.

'As long as you're sure.' At a loss for what else to say and feeling like the third wheel, he gathered the placemats and cutlery off the side and left them to it. He felt deeply uncomfortable. He could see why Nate was into her. She was gorgeous, but the fact that she was Monica's daughter made things very difficult. He hoped Tabatha was more careful with people's hearts than her mother.

The table was soon groaning under the feast that they had prepared. The young couple chatted and joked easily as they brought out the dishes, remarkably comfortable with each other in such a brief space of time.

'So, Tabatha. What's next for you now that you've finished university?' Jacob asked her as they sat down to eat.

'I'm trying to decide between going into teaching or taking a course in journalism,' she told him between mouthfuls of salad.

'Do you want a slice of quiche?' Nate asked, holding up the plate.

'Nuh uh.' she shook her head. 'I'm vegetarian. That has bacon in it.'

The look of horror on his son's face was a picture, and Jacob burst out laughing. He was still chuckling when he went to answer a knock at the door.

'Monica,' he said, startled, wiping his mouth with his napkin.

'Hello, Jacob. Is my daughter here by any chance? Gavin said he thought he saw her come this way.'

He looked down at her. The smudges of colour on her face and the ratty old t-shirt she was wearing were weirdly charming, and a surge of affection washed over him.

'Yes, she is. She's just outside with Nate.' He stood back, and she marched in, straight through the lounge and out to where the kids were still eating.

'Tabatha, what are you doing here?'

Tabatha half rose from her seat, then sat back down again. 'I'm having lunch,' she waved her fork to encompass the table. 'Us non-artistic types like to eat occasionally.'

Although Jacob could only see the back of her, he could tell Monica was bristling and ready to go full on mental at the girl, so he stepped in.

'Tabatha was kind enough to bring a book over for Nate,' he said smoothly, placing a hand on her arm. She looked up at him in shock, then down to where their skin touched. He could feel it, too. The tingling sensation that ran up his arm and fired his pulse rate into overdrive. He dropped his hand away quickly and coughed.

'Anyway, now you're here, why don't you join us?'

'No, I don't think...'

'Mum, have you eaten anything today?' Tabatha demanded, with a stern look on her features. Monica blew out a breath, looking upwards as if trying to remember. 'I thought as much,' the girl said, jumping up and guiding her to a seat. 'Sit there. I'll get another plate and stuff.'

Monica sat rigidly, staring at the tabletop, until Tabatha plonked a plate and cutlery in front of her and started spooning food onto it for her.

'Your daughter is quite a force,' Jacob joked to break the silence that had descended.

Monica looked at him, her eyes flashing. 'She's bossy is what she is!' But she threw a smile at Tabatha as she said it.

'I still can't believe you two knew each other all those years ago,' Tabatha said, taking her seat and picking up her fork. 'What was it, twenty years?'

'Twenty-two,' Jacob answered matter-of-factly. 'Actually, nearly twenty-three, just a few months shy.'

Monica's head shot up, and she stared at him, as if she couldn't believe he remembered.

'What?' he asked with a shrug. 'Can't a guy remember important events in his life?'

'So important that he buggered off without a backwards glance?' she snapped, her face flushing.

'That's rich coming from you,' he blurted before he could think about it. Where the hell did she get off being angry at him?

Their gazes were still locked, and the air seemed to crackle between them, with all the pain and passion that was resurfacing after all this time. He saw her eyes widen in shock, then drop down as she glanced around, finally noticing the open-mouthed gazes of the kids. She dropped her cutlery with a clatter and shoved back her chair.

'I'm sorry, this was a mistake...' She stood, then ran out of the villa.

Jacob propped his elbows on the table and leant his head on his hands, clutching it like it was going to fall off. Nothing she said made any damn sense. What the hell was going on?

NINETEEN

Tabatha crept back into their villa a short while later, unsure of her reception, but her mum smiled as she came out to the terrace. She picked up the wine bottle on the table and poured herself a glass, sitting down next to her.

'So, do you want to tell me what all that was about?' she asked quietly. Monica gave a brittle laugh and took a hefty slug from her glass.

'Not really, no.' She could tell Tabs was waiting for her to continue, but she couldn't. Instead, she waved a brochure and asked, 'so, are we going to arrange some spa treatments for my birthday tomorrow?'

Tabatha tilted her head, raking her face with her eyes, trying to discern what was going on there.

'OK,' she said, obviously giving up and snatching the brochure from her. 'What do you fancy?'

They spent a quiet afternoon by the pool. Tabatha was reading, casting occasional looks at her mum where she sat sketching endless variations of the view. As the evening drew in, they migrated inside to put on cardigans against the chill.

'Do you want to go out for dinner?' Tabatha asked her. 'Or shall we order in?'

'Actually, I've got a bit of a headache. You get yourself something from room service. I'm going to have an early night.'

Monica got ready for bed and curled up into a tight ball under the covers, finally allowing the tears that she'd been holding back all afternoon to spill out. That entire scene at Jacob's villa had been horrible. She wished she hadn't gone over. Trying to keep her sobs at a low volume, she pulled the cover over her head to block everything out.

The next morning, she looked at her reflection in the bathroom mirror with a scowl. It accurately reflected the image of a woman another year older. It also accurately reflected the image of a woman who, unable to sleep, had got up after her daughter went to bed and finished off the bottle of wine in a fit of pique. Her usually pale skin was almost translucent, the smudges under her eyes were vivid by contrast, and she was sure her crow's feet had deepened overnight. 'Happy bloody birthday, you silly old woman,' she told herself.

A sharp, insistent knocking on the front door pulled her away from her personal critique of her features, but the scowl remained in place as she flung the door open.

'Happy birthday!' exclaimed Gavin, looking far too buoyant for this time in the morning. He had one of the delivery trolleys with him, laden with an enormous bunch of flowers, piles of croissants, a jug of fresh orange juice and a bottle of Dom Pérignon nestled in an ice bucket.

'My goodness, thank you, Gavin. How did you know?'

'This was actually Sam's doing. He emailed me a few days ago.'

A fond smile flitted across her face. Of course it was Sam. Tabatha padded out in her robe, her hair tousled and eyes bleary.

'Morning Mum, happy birthday. What's all this?'

'Uncle Sam has arranged a little surprise. Looks like we're having mimosas and croissants for breakfast!'

Tabatha pushed her hair out of her eyes and grinned. 'Good. Let's start your celebrations as we mean to go on.' She reached past her mother, plucked a croissant off the plate, and stuffed it into her mouth, taking hold of the trolley, pulling it in with her other hand.

'There's another surprise lined up for you later on. Come over to the office after your spa treatments,' Gavin told her with a mischievous glint in his eyes. Monica looked back at Tabatha, an eyebrow arched in query, but her daughter held up both hands in denial, croissant still in her mouth. Buoyed by the surprise gestures, Monica found a genuine smile.

'Thank you, Gavin. We'll see you later.'

She joined Tabatha in the kitchen and took two champagne flutes out of the cupboard and poured the drinks.

'Cheers,' said Tabatha, raising her glass. 'And happy birthday again, Mum.'

They both took a sip and Monica watched as her daughter pulled a small package out of her bathrobe pocket, holding it out to her with a smile.

'Oh, you shouldn't have,' she said crossly, putting down her glass, but took it and carefully stripped off the pretty wrapping. When she opened the box inside, it revealed a silver necklace with a tiny, intricate artist's easel hanging from it.

'I love it', she said, reaching in to hug her. They got organised and took the birthday breakfast outside. It was another glorious day. The sun had already warmed the air, and as they sat enjoying the morning, Monica decided this birthday might not be so bad after all.

She was still on something of a champagne-fuelled high after the facials and manicures that they'd booked. They both had a quick shower and dressed before going over to see Gavin and discover what the other surprise might be. He led them out the back of the office, down a short corridor and into a dimly lit room. It was a small cinema room, with just two rows of plush blue seats and a large screen covering the far wall, lit up, paused on the opening shot of a film.

Monica sucked in a sharp breath. She didn't need to ask what it was. She'd seen that image of a light box being switched on more than a thousand times, every time she watched her favourite film.

'Oh goody, snacks,' Tabatha said, spotting the table next to the door and going to investigate. 'Who the hell drinks Vimto?' she asked her in disgust, holding one can aloft. *Monica Palmer when she was seventeen,* she thought. *I was addicted to the stuff.* Going to stand next to her daughter, she could see a big bowl of chocolate-covered raisins, another of nachos and yet another of popcorn. She didn't have to taste it to know it was salted caramel. All of her favourite, film-watching snacks. And there was only one person who could know all these details. One person, who despite the nearly twenty-three years they'd been apart, remembered that it was her birthday today and knew exactly what would make her smile.

She watched Funny Face in something of a daze, barely registering the familiar scenes that she knew by heart, and not correcting Tabatha's assumption that this was another of Sam's efforts. When it was over, she made her excuses and, with jittery steps, went to face her past.

TWENTY

'I think we need to talk,' Monica stated flatly when he answered the door. His heart fluttered unsteadily. Even though he had been expecting a response to his surprise, now that she was here, a moment of doubt spliced through him. What had he been thinking? He stared down at her. She looked paler than usual, despite several days of glorious French sunshine, making her appear more waif-like than ever. He glanced back inside to check Nate wasn't around.

'A simple thank you would suffice,' he replied gruffly, trying to keep a lid on the emotions bubbling up inside. She gave him a beatific smile that sent his pulse rate rocketing, her eyes never leaving his.

'I think we both know that we have unfinished business, as your wonderful birthday surprise showcased.'

He took a deep breath in through his nose. She was right, annoyingly. He couldn't deny his glee at setting it up for her, knowing how much she would appreciate the gesture and what it would mean to her. He let out the breath he'd been holding and nodded.

'Ok, but not here. How about I take you for dinner tonight?' He asked impulsively. Monica's eyes widened in astonishment and she considered him for a moment.

'Oh, why the hell not? If we're going to do this, we may as well do it in style,' she grinned with that impish gleam that he remembered so well. He found himself chuckling in response and checked the time.

'Shall we say seven o'clock?'

The drive up to St Paul De Vence and the restaurant that Gavin had recommended was filled with ill at ease conversations about everything but the issue at hand. The elephant that had been in the room sitting gaily in the back seat of the car, looking on with Machiavellian enjoyment. A vine covered archway led into the small, intimate space nestled in the ramparts of the town with just a few tables laid out with rich linens and gleaming glassware. Jacob was glad he'd taken Gavin's advice and booked ahead as they were led to the only empty table at the end of the row overlooking the old walls and the valley below.

The Maître d' fussed around them, pulling out their chairs and laying embroidered napkins on their laps before handing Jacob the wine menu. He scanned it quickly, then looked across the table at her.

'Do you fancy some red? They've got a great Malbec.'

'I prefer white,' she told him. Of course she did, he thought crossly. He hated white wine and couldn't tolerate it even to be polite.

'Well, I can't drink that,' he said, his nose wrinkling in distaste.

'So, get one of each,' she gave a carefree shrug and a grin. 'It is my birthday, after all.'

Once the wine had been served, tasted, and approved, the waiter scurried off with a promise to return shortly and they sat in silence for a while.

'So...' he said, not sure where to start. It was so surreal to be sitting here with her. Confronting Monica was a scenario that had played through his mind many times over the years, but now it was happening he was at a loss at what to say. Part of him didn't want to spoil the evening, the other part was desperate for answers.

Monica put her glass down carefully on the table, rolling its stem between her fingers, her eyes trained on the swirling contents. Without taking her eyes from her wine, she asked quietly, 'why did you never answer my letters?' When he didn't respond straight away, her eyes slid up to look at him.

'What the hell are you talking about, Mon? You never answered mine. I wrote to you every week for a year and not once did you respond. Not even to say goodbye.' His voice choked at the end of the sentence and he took a sip of wine to swallow down the grief. The hand on the glass stilled, and she was staring at him in shock, her mouth open in wordless disbelief.

'Well, that's just not possible,' she finally hissed, her eyebrows scrunched together, a line appearing between them. Jacob slumped back in his chair, his mind racing. She looked genuinely perplexed, but he didn't know if he could believe her.

'So, you wrote to me?'

She nodded vigorously. 'I did. Not for an entire year, but for a few months,' she admitted, looking at him through her lashes, her face still creased in confusion.

'Well, if you wrote, and I wrote, but neither of us saw any letters, then...' he trailed off.

'Then it doesn't take a rocket scientist to work out our parents had a hand in this debacle,' she finished angrily, picking up her glass again. He couldn't quite believe it, but memories were surfacing. His dad saying, "never mind, son, there's plenty more fish in the sea" and other such triteness, his mother agreeing fervently and declaring he was too good for that chit of a girl. At the time, he'd assumed they were just trying to be supportive. But now? Now he was going to have a whole lot of words with them when he got back. How could they have watched him suffer like that?

He looked back at Monica, who was obviously having similar thoughts by the scowl on her face.

'I guess this changes things,' he told her. She blinked rapidly at his words. He could almost see the thoughts racing through her mind, and he smiled gently at her.

'I'm not sure it changes much,' she said with a sniff and finished her wine. He picked up the bottle of chardonnay and topped up her glass.

'It might not change the past, but it changes the now, doesn't it?' he asked as he poured.

'Maybe,' she replied uncertainly, her soulful blue eyes spearing his when he looked up. He couldn't remember her ever looking doubtful about anything. She'd always been so sure about everything when they were young, her confidence evident in everything she said or did. It had been inspiring to be around.

He put the bottle down and raised his glass towards her. 'Here's to new beginnings?'

'To new beginnings,' she parroted, an awestruck look lighting up her face.

TWENTY-ONE

The waiter returned to take their orders and Monica hastily glanced through the menu, picking something at random, her mind still too appalled at the revelation that Jacob had written to her. He had wanted to stick to their plan and not let the distance get in the way of their love. He'd tried for an entire year, whereas she had given up after a few months. After the letter telling him she was carrying their baby. There seemed little point when even that shocking news elicited no reply.

'Tell me about your life, Mon. I'd like to know what I have missed.'

She gave an unladylike sort, nearly shooting a mouthful of wine through her nose. Not bothering to correct him about her name, she dabbed her nose with the napkin.

'There's not much to tell, really.'

'Come on! There's your painting. You obviously followed that passion. And there's your daughter. Were you married?'

'No, I never married,' she said hesitantly. 'But yes, painting has been my life. That's why I'm here, actually. I'm looking for inspiration. I have a big show coming up. How about you?'

'You mean about being married or about being here?' he shifted in his seat, not quite able to meet her gaze.

'Both, I guess?'

'Yes. Yes, I was married, but she passed away eighteen months ago.' His eyes came back up to meet hers and she could see clouds of pain in them. Reaching out, she laid a hand over his on the table and gave it a squeeze.

'I'm truly sorry, Jacob.'

He gave a small nod of thanks, pulling his hand away quickly and picking his wine up. 'That's mostly why I'm here. Sarah and I used to holiday in France all the time, and Nate... Well, Nate has been struggling since she died. I'm hoping this vacation, sorry, *holiday*, will help snap him out of it.'

She smiled at his correction. 'I still can't believe you remembered Funny Face is my favourite film,' she told him, deciding a change of topic was the safest option.

'How could I forget? You made me watch the damn thing so many times I used to have dreams about Audrey Hepburn!'

She laughed at the memories of him protesting vociferously each time, even though they both knew he'd let her watch whatever she wanted in the end.

'I let you watch Roman Holiday occasionally! Do you remember, we were going to go to Rome, hire a Vespa and re-enact that scene?'

He let out a loud guffaw, a grin creasing his face, his green eyes lighting up with amusement. 'There's no way in hell I would have let you drive. I never told you that.'

She threw a mock scowl at him. 'As if you could've stopped me.'

They smiled at each other for a moment, their old intimacy reappearing just like that, even after two long decades. The rest of the evening passed easily, memory lane providing an abundance of things to talk about that were safe topics as far as Monica was concerned. All the time, as they laughed and reminisced over the antics they used to get up to, there was a nagging voice in the back of her mind.

Tell him. Tell him he has a daughter, and Nate has a half-sister. You have to tell him. But she couldn't seem to find the right moment or the courage and before she knew it, they were on their way back to the villas.

There was a weird moment when they got back. Monica had had a sense that Jacob was going to kiss her goodnight, and when he reached in to give her what turned out to be a hug, she'd darted out of range, leaving him hanging awkwardly.

'So, that was fun,' she said brightly, feeling awkward now, away from the surreal, intimate setting of the restaurant and firmly back in reality.

'Maybe we can do it again sometime?'

Her mind was whirling with a desire to see him again, but mixed with the fear that she'd have to tell him the truth. And if she did that, she would have to admit to Tabatha that she'd lied.

'Maybe. Goodnight, Jacob.'

She hurried to her villa before he could respond, diving through the door with relief. She needed time to process this.

'I'm home Tabs,' she called as she walked in, then stopped in shock, her blood running cold. Tabatha was stretched out on the sofa with Nate, her legs casually over his lap. They looked far too familiar and comfortable.

'It's probably time you went home now, Nate,' she snapped, pulling off her jacket. Tabatha looked up in annoyance, but Nate obediently moved her legs and stood up.

'Why does he have to go?' Tabatha stood next to him, looking at her defiantly.

'It's ok. I should probably get back,' he mumbled, eyes lowered as he made haste to the door.

'What was that?' Tabatha asked as soon as it closed behind him.

'Don't you think he's a bit young for you?' Monica stammered, heading to the fridge and pulling out the wine even though she knew she'd already had plenty. She couldn't think straight. This was all just too much to cope with, and oblivion beckoned.

'I'm not a kid, you know? I am quite capable of deciding who I hang out with. Anyway, we're just friends.'

'Hmm. Well, I just don't think hanging out with him is a good idea.'

'You are being impossible! I'm going to bed, but this conversation is not over.'

Tabatha flounced to her bedroom, forcefully shutting the door to let her mother know how pissed off she was. *You might not be a kid, but you're not quite an adult yet,* she thought as she took her wine outside. She tried calling Sam, but it went straight to voicemail so she sent him a text instead.

Everything is a mess. Need your input asap! Xx

Staring up at the starlit sky, she didn't know what she should do for the best. Could she keep this from them both, now that she knew the truth about Jacob's disappearance from her life? Or was it better to let sleeping dogs lie? After all, Tabatha had grown up thinking her father wasn't around and didn't seem any less well-balanced for that fact. The pros and cons twisted in her brain. She knew what the right thing to do was; it was obvious, but would Tabatha ever forgive her for her years of fabrication?

TWENTY-TWO

Jacob was feeling uncommonly light-hearted, despite the awkward end to their evening. Knowing that Monica hadn't ignored him all that time ago was a bigger salve to his soul than he could have imagined. A part of him that had been broken now felt almost healed by the discovery, leaving him at peace with that chapter of his life. Although he was angry as hell at his parents, and hers for that matter, as they must have been integral in the duplicity, he felt remarkably benevolent towards them, buoyed by the evening he'd just shared with her.

It was like no time had passed. She could still make him laugh like a hyena, and make his blood race and temperature rise at the same time. The way her eyes flashed in delight tonight, when she said something witty, and her face had lit up at his responses, seemed to indicate that she felt the same way. That she still wanted to be the one to make him smile. Where they went from here, he had no idea, but he felt a buzz of excitement at the thought of finding out. He just had to think of how to convince her to go out again.

'Hey, champ,' he called as Nate came through the door. He flicked his eyes at him, a sullen look on his face.

'Oh, hey, Dad.' Jacob watched as he slouched into the kitchen, glanced inside the fridge and then shut the door again with a huff of irritation.

'What's up?'

'Nothing. Did you have fun tonight?'

He couldn't help the smile that burst onto his face, but he tried to keep the excitement out of his voice. 'Yeah, I did. It was good to catch up with Monica.'

'Do you like her? I mean, like her, like her?'

A denial sprung to his lips, but he'd always prided himself on never lying to his son, so he swiftly rethought his answer.

'Truth be told, I do. I always did. We went out for a while when I lived in London.'

Nate sniffed as he digested this information, biting his lower lip. 'What about Mum?'

Jacob walked over and placed his hand on his shoulders, looking down at him as he spoke. 'This fact doesn't affect how much I loved your mum, Nate.'

A flash of pain crossed the boy's face. Instinctively, he pulled him in close, wrapping his arms around the slender frame and holding it tightly. Nate tolerated the gesture for a second, then pulled away, ducking his head and surreptitiously rubbing his eyes.

'What's the plan for tomorrow?'

'How about we just relax? Stay here, soak up some rays and chill?'

Nate's hand flew to his mouth, and he widened his eyes in mock horror. 'Jacob Riley sitting still for five minutes? Am I hearing things?'

'Hilarious. But I figured it won't hurt. We've been out every day so far.'

'I've been telling you that from the start.'

Jacob was happy to see his son's demeanour had reverted to its boyish, fun side of the last few days and clapped him on the shoulder affectionately.

'Well, now I'm taking your advice. On that note, I'm going to bed. I'll see you in the morning.'

In the privacy of his room, he got changed and lay in his bed, feeling slightly guilty because he knew one reason he wanted to hang around the villa was to increase the chances of bumping into Monica. He felt like a giddy teenager again, in the first flushes of infatuation. It was completely ridiculous. Grinning to himself, he picked up his Kindle in the hope he could focus on something else long enough to get some sleep.

He was still smiling when he awoke in the early hours of the morning, but the cold light of day tempered the reality. Yes, it was fun, this intoxicating buzz, especially as he could never have imagined feeling it again just a few days ago. He padded through to the kitchen to turn on the coffee machine to warm, leaning against the counter as he thought things through.

Maybe I'm getting ahead of myself? The truth of the matter was they were both here on holiday, they lived thousands of miles apart, and there were decades between what they had as teenagers and now. He was an adult and had no excuses for flights of fancy about a woman who had so shockingly reappeared in his world. He had a life, responsibilities, a son. Monica had been right to hesitate when he'd suggested going out again. She was obviously more judicious in her thinking.

Although he'd promised Nate he would relax, he couldn't not exercise, so settled for a few laps of the pool while the coffee was being made, rather than his usual eight-mile run. Astonished to find Nate up and ensconced on the sofa when he came back in, he did a comic double take.

'This is one for the record books,' he said, with an exaggerated look at his watch. 'Nate Riley voluntarily up before nine!'

Nate gave him a sardonic half grin and waved his phone. 'I got a message from Tabatha. It woke me.'

Jacob, senses heightened, asked as casually as he could, 'oh, yes? What are they up to today?'

His son stretched and yawned, taking a maddeningly long time to respond. 'Her mum's dragged her off to some market. In Italy?' he queried. 'Are we that close?'

'Yeah, we're not too far from the border,' he replied, his heart lurching with disappointment as he went into the kitchen. That sounded like an all day thing, so she would not be around. As he poured his coffee, he realised that all the rational thinking in the world was pointless. He could reason with himself as much as he liked, but the cold hard truth was he still had feelings for Monica.

TWENTY - THREE

'No!' exclaimed Sam when she told him the sorry saga the next morning. 'You mean to tell me that both of your parents decided you shouldn't be together? And you said your life wasn't a soap opera.'

'I know, it's crazy, right? I just don't know what to do.'

'Well, honey, take your time. You don't have to rush into anything after all these years.'

'I don't know, Sam. Delaying telling them just compounds the situation in the long run.'

'Hmm. Maybe, but you can be forgiven for taking a little time. Why don't you take Tabatha out for the day, go off somewhere? Perhaps sound her out about the whole *actually* having a dad idea?'

'That's a possibility,' she mused. 'It also keeps her away from Nate. Despite what she said last night, I'm not sure he thinks they're just friends. And I don't want to think about those consequences.'

'Oh, I don't think you have any concerns in that department,' he said ambiguously.

Monica took a sip of her coffee, considering the options. 'You know, I saw an excursion in the villa book to this wonderful, quaint looking market just over the border, on the Italian side.'

'That sounds fabulous, I wish I could come.'

'Well, get your arse over here, Sam, I told you before.'

He went quiet for a moment. 'I'm thinking about it. I probably will... You know me, I'll have a sudden mad urge and jump on a plane.'

'Well, I hope you do, and soon!'

Flicking through the pages of the villa book, Monica found the excursion she was thinking of. It looked perfect, a full day private tour to Ventimiglia. The pictures showed a colourful old town with a bustling, substantial market that would take hours to explore. She nodded and picked up her phone, *was it too early to call Gavin?* She considered the screen for a moment. Not wanting to wake him, she opted to send a message instead, thinking it was less invasive. But she needn't have worried, as an answer pinged straight back. The man evidently was never off duty.

Once the details were confirmed, she made Tabs a cup of her favourite herbal tea and went to wake her, hoping she would be in a better mood this morning.

'Tabs,' she called softly, placing the cup on the bedside table and sitting on the edge of the bed. 'Tabs,' she said again, a little louder and giving her shoulder a gentle shake.

Tabatha snuffled and rolled over, opening one eye to look at her as she grunted, 'what?'

Still in a bad mood then, Monica thought with a sigh. 'I've made you tea.'

When this elicited no further response, she added, 'I just wanted to apologise for last night.'

The other eye opened and Tabatha pushed herself upright, watching her guardedly.

'I just don't understand why you were being so weird about Nate.' She reached for the tea and clasped the cup between both hands.

'I'm sorry, love. I was just tired, that's all. Must have been all the birthday excitement.'

'I think it has more to do with whatever has gone on, or is going on between Jacob and you,' she said astutely, taking a sip.

Monica stared at her for a moment. Should she just tell her now and get it over with? Her heart quailed at the thought and instead she said cheerily, 'to make up for it, I've arranged a trip for us today.'

Tabatha bucked up at this news, the vestiges of her bad mood falling away. 'That's more like it! What are we doing?'

'We are going to Italy,' she told her grandly as she stood. 'So you need to get yourself up and dressed.'

Looking delighted, Tabatha put the cup down and pulled off the covers. 'Wow, ok. How long have I got?'

'We're being picked up in an hour, so you have time for breakfast,' she smiled at her. 'Oh, and don't forget your passport.'

As promised by the pictures, Ventimiglia was a charming old town with a host of market stalls lined up along the waterfront. Monica and Tabatha were soon immersed in the vibrant stalls, comparing sunglasses and cashmere scarfs, and debating the authenticity of designer handbags with prices too good to be true. They sampled homemade limoncello, fresh cheeses, and salamis before being distracted by a table of fabulous shoes, both treating themselves to a pair of sandals.

When their excitement began to flag, they searched for the perfect spot for lunch, finding an enchanting pizzeria tucked away on one of the back streets. It was a small family-run place with a traditional wood-fired oven in one corner where you could watch your pizzas being baked, and the smells coming from there were heavenly. The umber, colour-washed walls were punctuated with black and white family photographs depicting the restaurant over the years, adding to the homely atmosphere.

'Oh, this has been such fun,' Tabatha said, sitting back once they'd ordered. Monica smiled at her, glad there was no trace of her previous rancour. 'It certainly has. And I've taken loads of photos. I think some of the market stalls might make excellent subjects for my paintings.'

'That's a great idea,' she replied, her gaze on the corner of the room. Monica glanced over, and saw a young girl of around five, tugging on the shirt of the cook. He looked down, beaming as he said something while he placed the paddle with pizzas into the fiery pit. That done, he wiped his hands on his apron and scooped her up high, her squeals of excitement sounding around the room.

'That's cute,' Tabatha observed, and Monica looked at her sharply.

'Do you ever feel like you missed out on not having a dad around?'

Monica held her breath as she watched her daughter consider the question. 'It's hard to say,' she said, nodding her thanks to the waiter who brought their wine. 'I never knew any difference, and let's face it, you are more than enough to make up for ten absent parents with your constant worrying about me.'

She gave a cheeky grin and a salute with her wine glass. 'But I guess it would have been nice,' she mused. 'You know, maybe to have another input, another perspective on things.'

Monica didn't say a word. She just absorbed what Tabs was saying and added it to her internal debate.

'Why, is it something that you beat yourself up about?' she asked her suddenly. 'I mean, it's hardly your fault he was gone before I was born.'

She returned her daughter's serious look, the words on the tip of her tongue but refusing to budge. 'No, I just wondered, that's all,' she said finally, dropping her eyes to the glass gripped in her hand. 'Look, I think those are ours,' she said, pointing over to the oven where the chef was pulling out two pizzas, all the while cursing herself for being such a coward.

TWENTY - FOUR

The idea came to him the next day when he was scrolling through a webpage for things to do in the area. The annoying adverts that had been following him around the internet ever since he'd first searched St Paul De Vence, finally proving useful. With a grin, Jacob picked up his phone. He knew without a doubt that the one way to get Monica to do something was to offer up a challenge.

Later that morning, he rapped on her door and waited patiently for her to answer. It took a while, but he knew through his surreptitious questioning of Nate that Monica was painting today. He also knew that his son had gone for a walk with Tabatha, so at least he wouldn't have an audience if this went horribly wrong and she refused.

When the door opened, she blinked in surprise to see him standing there. 'What do you want?' She asked, poking him with a pencil. 'I'm busy, as you can see.' She waved a hand down at her paint-stained t-shirt and went to shut the door.

He dangled a key on a large silver fob in the gap. 'I wondered if you fancied a trip out?'

She peered inquisitively at him, past the fob, and he took the opportunity to push the door back open so she could see the Vespa parked outside. A huge smile broke out on her face, but she still seemed hesitant.

'Of course, I still won't let you drive. But we can have some fun.'

As he'd expected, her response was immediate. She snatched the key off of him and walked into the lounge, calling over her shoulder. 'Let me change my top, and then I will take us for a drive.'

Jacob was actually taken aback and slightly relieved by how confident she seemed on the moped. One of his worries about this plan was that they'd end up in a tangled heap somewhere, but it looked like he was in expert hands. His arms flew around her waist and stayed there as they shot out of the drive and onto the main road leading up to the village.

'You've done this before,' he shouted into her ear as she manoeuvred easily through the traffic. Monica turned her head slightly to nod, eyes still on the road. 'I used to have a moped back in the day. I couldn't afford a car, you know, poor starving artist and all that.'

He tried to imagine this younger version of her that he hadn't known and realised he desperately wanted to fill in all the gaps. He'd missed out on so much and she hadn't really told him much about her life after he left, but he was determined to get her to open up. As they approached the village, she aimed the bike towards the entrance. 'I don't think we're allowed to take this in there,' he called urgently, but Monica just let out a whoop and sped up. Chuckling to himself, Jacob knew he should have known better, and he held on tightly to her waist as they zig-zagged through the pedestrians, followed by shouts of alarm and French curses.

When she finally slewed to a stop near the cafe where he'd seen her the other day, she was laughing as they got off. Monica's face was flushed with excitement, her blue eyes sparkling with glee as she took off her helmet and ran a hand through her long hair to straighten it out. He stared at her, dumbstruck by her beauty, as he fumbled at the clasp on his helmet.

'Here, let me,' she said and stepped forward, reaching up to help and standing impossibly close. He sucked in an urgent breath, fighting his increasing need to kiss her. The last thing he wanted to do was spoil things by rushing in like a fool.

'That was fun,' she told him with a smile. 'I needed a break, thank you.'

'More terrifying than fun from where I was sitting,' he joked, looking around. 'Lunch?'

'I could eat a little,' she admitted, pulling her bag from under the seat. 'I could also use a glass of wine, too, so you'll have to do the driving on the way back.'

'I won't argue with that,' he grinned at her and led the way to a free table at the cafe. The air was vibrant with multilingual conversations as the tourists enjoyed their lunch in the dazzling afternoon sun, and they sat in companionable silence as they waited to get served, soaking up the atmosphere.

'What's Nate up to today?' she asked once they'd placed their order.

'He's out for a walk with Tabatha, didn't you know?' he frowned, surprised that she was unaware. He saw her face darken for a split second, then a half smile appeared.

'She may have said something. I was probably lost in my painting at the time.' There was a peculiar expression on her face, as if she had something to say, but she remained quiet, so he filled the void.

'How is the painting going? You said something about a show coming up?'

Brightening up considerably, she reached forward and picked up her wine. 'Yes, Sam had organised a wonderful opportunity for me to showcase at the Tate. He's really outdone himself this time. I just hope I can do it justice.'

A flash of something that could have been jealousy shot through him. 'Sam being?' he asked, trying to sound like a normal person, not a green-eyed kid.

'He's my agent. He's also my oldest and best friend. In fact, you may get the chance to meet him. I've been trying to convince him to come out for a few days.'

This did nothing to answer the question he really wanted to know the answer to, but before he could probe further, a large platter was placed on the table overflowing with the mixed starters they had chosen. Crusty bread and olives, baked brie with pesto, smoked salmon, chicken liver pâté and cheesy gougères fought for space on the bed of mixed salad leaves.

They both stared at it, then at each other, and burst into laughter. 'Just a light lunch then,' he scoffed, pushing the platter towards her.

'I think we may have overdone it a tad,' she agreed, selecting a piece of bread and smearing a scoop of pâté onto it. She took an enormous bite and let out a moan of pleasure which sent his pulse rate rocketing. Now there was a sound he would like to be responsible for. He just needed to find out if she felt the same way or if this Sam she talked about was already holding that position.

TWENTY - FIVE

Monica couldn't quite understand the expression on Jacob's face when she talked about Sam. There was something there, almost a look of dislike. But the food arrived, and she dived in to scoop up some pâté, letting the wonderful taste and texture come out in a groan of pleasure. She'd spent far too long denying herself these simple pleasures, but France seemed to be freeing up her reticence and allowing her to enjoy everything. Or maybe it was Jacob having that effect on her.

His surprise arrival with the Vespa had allowed her to regress. To leap into the moment, become that free-spirited, wanton youth that didn't give a monkey's about what people thought or what she should do and who could just go with the flow. It felt wonderful.

'So, how is your family? Your parents and Genie? Oh God, and Caleb, how's he doing?' she asked through an amazing mouthful of brie.

Jacob's face stilled. It was as if all the light had left him, leaving a caricature of a serious-looking adult instead of the boyishly handsome man she'd sat down to lunch with. The temperature dropped around them, and she struggled to finish her mouthful.

'What? What happened to Caleb?'

Jacob took a slug of water but looked like he wished it were something stronger.

'He went to the bad when we got home,' he told her as he stared at his empty glass. 'Started out with pilfering from local shops. Got in with the wrong crowd.' His eyes slid up to meet hers and the pain there was unbearable. She sucked in a breath, knowing this story didn't have a happy ending. 'One night, he and his gang decided to rob an all-night store.' He gave a chuckle that was without any trace of humour in it. 'Just some cans of coke and cigarettes, that's all they were after. But the store owner had other ideas. He shot him. He shot my little brother dead for some soda and some Marlborough's.'

Monica shoved her plate aside and stood, reaching over to Jacob to take him in her arms. She could remember Caleb vividly, a cheeky little boy who admired his big brother, and she knew, despite his disparaging comments back then, that Jacob loved the boy beyond measure. As his head rested against her chest, she struggled to find the words.

'Fuck me, you haven't had much luck, have you?'

Jacob let out a noise that she thought was a sob, but it turned into a guffaw of laughter which reverberated through her chest.

'You could say that,' he said, looking up at her, a hand wiping away an errant tear. As their eyes met, Monica knew that he was going to kiss her, more certainly than she knew her daughter's birthday.

'I have to tell you something,' she said urgently, pulling back.

'Mon,' he said, gently placing a finger on her lips. 'It can wait.'

And he reached up, bringing his lips to hers, and the world exploded around her. It was familiar, yet strange, and blew everything she'd experienced since he'd left out of the water. She sagged against him, 'Jacob, I...'

He grabbed the back of her head, pulling her in again and roving deeper with his tongue, his hands roaming through her hair, then slipping down her back. Monica pulled on all the strength she had and drew away.

'I think we need to take a step back,' she breathed, sitting back in her chair. They stared at each other for a moment.

'Why?' he asked, adjusting himself in his chair to accommodate his reaction to kissing her.

'Because,' she replied, taking a grateful sip from her glass.

'Because, what?' he asked, his eyes still clouded with lust, the lids heavy as he looked at her. He bit his lower lip then grinned, tilting his head, waiting for an answer.

'Because I said so?' she jested, sure that he had used the same response to his kid at some point. He leant back, eyes still locked on hers, and inhaled deeply before nodding.

'Fair enough.' He sat back upright, forking up some salmon and lettuce onto his plate, and beginning to eat.

Monica looked at him, taken aback. 'Is that it?'

'Is that what?' he mumbled through a mouthful of food, picking up the napkin to wipe his chin.

'Is that... I mean...' she ran out of words, her mind still reeling from the kiss.

He grinned, his dimple playing havoc with her heart. 'If you mean, is that the end of me pushing further than you want to go right now, then yes. Of course. But if you mean, is that the end of me trying to convince you we should investigate this bizarre reunion and see if it leads anywhere, then definitely not.'

'Oh,' she said quietly. At a loss for what else to say, she picked up her fork and started to eat. She was totally confused. The feelings she had towards Jacob now were diametrically opposite to how she felt about him when she landed in France. She'd hated him for years for breaking her heart, and even now, knowing the truth, part of her couldn't quite trust him. But equally, she couldn't deny the attraction she felt towards him. If anything, it was greater now than it had been.

Good looks aside, he was confident, kind, and thoughtful, despite what he had been through. It took strength to be like that, and she admired that and found it extremely alluring. The few men she'd had relationships with over the years hadn't managed to pull that off. If they were confident, they were cocky as hell and usually self-centred, and the artist in her needed attention. If they were kind and thoughtful, she'd perceived them as weak, and ultimately, they were no match for her bolshy personality.

She was getting the sense that Jacob had grown into a man who combined all of the best traits, as well as being able to set her body aflame with a simple kiss, and it was absolutely terrifying.

TWENTY - SIX

Trying to focus on his food was damn near impossible, but Jacob knew he had to give Monica some space. So, he ate on, casually throwing glances at her as they chatted about this and that, nothing heavy, nothing of consequence, as they finished their lunch. But his insides were churning, still fizzing with his response to the kiss. The deep wound left by the unnecessary death of his kid brother was still raw, and talking about it was tough, but when Monica had embraced him all he could think about was kissing her there and then.

It had been out of this world, an explosion of supernova proportions shooting through his body leaving an effervescent glow. And now all he could think about was doing it again. When there was a natural lull in the conversation, he took a deep breath.

'Look, Mon, I know this is all a bewildering situation,' he gestured between them. 'But as we both know, if it wasn't for our parents interfering, we would have stayed in touch. Now, of course, I have no idea where that would have gone. For all I know, we might have gotten bored with each other before a few months had passed, but I honestly doubt it.' He looked at her, seeing if she was going to rebut that statement, but she remained quiet, eyes trained on her fingers fiddling with the napkin on the table.

'Don't you think we owe it to ourselves to see if there is something here?'

She looked at him sharply then, went to say something but abruptly took another drink of wine before talking.

'Jacob, there is obviously something here, but I think we are both old enough now not to get carried away by physical attraction, don't you?' There was a trace of bitterness in her voice that he couldn't fathom. Somebody in her past must have hurt her badly, he thought, even though her words stung. Did she really think this was just physical?

'I don't believe this is just physical, and I think you know that.'

'Damn it, Jacob,' her hand slapped the table. 'Why are you so gungho to drag all of this up?' She stood as if she was going to leave, pulling her bag from the back of her chair, then looking about, muttering under her breath.

He held up the keys to the Vespa with a grin. 'Going somewhere?' She gave him a deathly glare, but he kept his smile going. He didn't know why she was fighting this, but he was determined to find out. 'Sit down, Mon. Finish your wine, then I'll take you back.' It felt good to have the upper hand with her for once.

'I could call Gavin to come and get me,' she pouted, but sat anyway.

'For sure, you could. But I don't think you want to.'

She frowned into her wineglass. He could see some kind of internal struggle going on in her head, and just sat back and waited it out. Training college kids for ten years had taught him lots of things, patience being the predominant one.

'There are things you don't know,' she said finally. 'Something that will change how you feel about all of this.'

'Are you a serial killer?'

Her face softened, and a giggle escaped her lips. 'No, don't be silly.'

'Well, that's about the only thing that I'd object to.'

'We'll see,' she told him, staring off into the distance for a moment before returning her focus to him. 'I'll have to think about it. About telling you. There are other people this affects.'

'Colour me confused,' he jested, but nodded. And he was confused. He had no idea what she was talking about or what could make any difference with what was going on between them unless she was involved with her agent. 'In the meantime, how about we go for dinner tomorrow? I'm sure Nate won't mind ordering another pizza. I'm assuming Tabatha will feel the same way as long as it's veggie?'

'I'm not sure that's a good idea.'

'It's just dinner, Mon. We're not eloping!'

She smiled then, a simple upturn of her lips that brought him hope. 'Look, let me give you my number and you can let me know what you decide. No pressure, see?'

She slid her phone across the table, and he tapped in his number with a grin. 'Right, come on then. Let's get you back, I believe you have some painting to do.'

He relished the feel of her arms around him as they drove back, and he wished the journey was longer. When they pulled up, he dipped his head and kissed her chastely on the cheek. 'Let me know,' he said simply, and turned to walk to his villa, resisting the urge to look back.

Inside, he gave a muted whoop of glee and went to get a well-deserved beer. Surprised that Nate hadn't returned, he made a note to tease him about his new found joy of walking, then went to lay by the pool. When his phone rang, he saw it was his sister, and guiltily let it go to voicemail. There was no way he could talk to Genie right now knowing she wouldn't have anything good to say about Monica. He didn't want to burst this bubble of happiness. She could know about it *if and when* there was something to tell.

While he was thinking about where he would take Mon tomorrow if she said yes, Nate finally mooched in.

'The wanderer returns,' he called out to him, standing to go inside.

'Hi, Dad. Cool bike outside, is that ours?'

He clapped him on the shoulder. 'It certainly is. Do you want to take your girlfriend for a spin?' he asked jovially. Nate flushed and mumbled, 'she's not my girlfriend. We're just friends.'

'Aw, sorry bud. Have you been stuck in the friendzone?'

Nate shrugged his hand away sulkily. 'Dad, really? We get on well, that's all, and she's just finished at Oxford. We've got tons to talk about. It is possible for a girl and a boy to hang out as friends, you know?'

'Ok, ok, sorry. I didn't mean to upset you. Do you fancy a game of handball in the pool?'

'Sure, let me get my swim shorts on.'

Feeling sorry for Nate and his unrequited love, he checked his phone, but there were no new messages. Hopefully he wouldn't find himself feeling the same way as his son tomorrow.

TWENTY - SEVEN

'I don't know what to do, Sam,' Monica said as she paced the terrace. 'I can't ignore what there is between us, but I don't know if I'm ready to tell Tabs.'

There was a pause on the line, and she stopped as she waited for his wisdom. 'The way I see it Monica, you'll have to tell them both. The longer you leave it, the harder it will be. Rip the Band-Aid off and see what bleeds.'

'Charming,' she giggled. 'But I know you're right.'

She saw Tabatha coming in and said quickly, 'I have to go, she's back. I'll talk to you later.'

'Hi, Mum,' Tabatha called as she came out, dropping onto a chair. 'How has your day been?'

'Interesting,' she replied, wondering where to start. 'How was your walk? You didn't say you were going with Nate.'

'That's because you get all weird about him. Anyway, how do you know that?'

Monica sighed and sat opposite her. 'Jacob came over. We went for lunch, actually.'

Tabatha gave her an appraising look. 'Did you now? You want to tell me what's going on there?' She was grinning like the proverbial Cheshire cat and obviously had a good idea.

'Only if you tell me what's going on with you and Nate,' she said swiftly, hoping against all the odds it was innocent.

'I told you, Mum. We're just friends. He's a sweet boy and we share a love of literature. We get on well.' Her face was a picture of honesty, but colour had risen to her cheeks as if there was more to tell.

'Well, just make sure it stays that way.'

Tabatha snorted, pushing her errant hair out of her eyes. 'You're being absurd.'

'Why am I? As far as I know, you haven't been out with a boy for years. I realise you've been focused on uni, which is great, but it's not beyond the realm of possibility that you might be up for a holiday fling.'

'I could say the same for you! When was the last time you had a relationship?'

'Touché. Anyway, it's complicated with Jacob. I'm not sure there's any point to it.'

Tabatha stood up. 'I don't see why. He seems like a nice guy and you clearly like him or we wouldn't be having this conversation. Why don't you just see how it goes? No pressure.'

The repetition of the words Jacob had used earlier jolted her. Tabatha was so like him, it was ridiculous. She hadn't seen it before, or hadn't wanted to, but it was undeniable.

'Tabatha, I have to tell you something about him,' she started with a surge of courage, but was interrupted when a phone rang. Tabatha pulled her phone out of her pocket and her face lit up when she saw who was calling. Monica's heart fluttered in panic, but her fears were allayed when she answered it.

'Hi, Sally. Just a sec.' She held the phone to her chest. 'I'm going to take this in my room, Mum.'

Monica nodded and watched as her daughter started talking animatedly as she walked back into the villa and out of sight. Relief flooded her that the conversation had been postponed. Maybe this was a sign that she should wait. Latching on to that idea, even though she knew it was cowardly, she went to change back into her painting clothes. I should go out with him again and see if he really is the good guy he seems to be, she rationalised. That way, I can decide if he is someone who deserves Tabatha in his life. Convincing herself that this was the sensible solution, she sent him a quick message agreeing to tomorrow night.

Ignoring the uneasiness vibrating in her stomach, she tied up her hair and got the paints out. As her brush hit the canvas, the memory of his lips claiming hers flashed before her and she shivered in delight. God, it had been amazing. Nobody had ever made her body react the way Jacob did. If anything, it was more potent now. Her hand flew across the canvas, bright colours flowing from the brush as she lost herself in the process, completely absorbed, her problems momentarily vanishing.

She had no idea how long she'd been working when Tabatha came back out.

'Wow, that's remarkable,' she said, coming over for a closer look. She tilted her head. 'What is it, fireworks?'

Coming out of her trance, Monica stepped back and looked at what had appeared like magic. She had never understood how these images flowed out of her when she found her "zen" as she liked to call it.

'It's more of a feeling,' she told her, wiping her brush and laying it on the palette. 'How's Sally?'

Tabatha's face fell into a frown. 'Not so good. Her mum's not very well. I was hoping she might be able to join us for a couple of days but it doesn't look like that's going to happen.'

'I'm sorry, love. It would have been fun to have your friend visit, you two are usually joined at the hip!'

'Yes, we are,' she said wistfully, staring at a point on the horizon. Monica leaned in and gave her a hug.

'Listen, I've agreed to go out with Jacob tomorrow night. Why don't you make a plan with your friend Nate?'

Her daughter chuckled. 'Thanks, Mum. He's no Sally, but yeah, we could do something. I might see if Gavin will let us watch something in that funky little cinema he's got.'

'That's the spirit. I tell you what, shall we order in something yummy from room service and pamper ourselves with some of those products in the bathrooms? Have a girlie night?'

'Want to make yourself beautiful for your date?' she grinned.

'It's not a date!'

'Oh, really? Then what is it?' she laughed as she went to get the menu. *I have no idea*, Monica thought as she waited for her to return. *But hopefully by the end of it, I will.*

TWENTY - EIGHT

It was dusk when Jacob went to collect Monica. The kids had left earlier, having organised a binge-watching session of their favourite films. He was glad that Nate had found a friend in Tabatha. It would make things easier if this thing with Mon led somewhere and lasted beyond their time in France. Although how that would look, he couldn't imagine. *Stop overthinking,* he chided himself as he rapped smartly on her door.

When it opened, the sight of her sucked the breath out of him. Wearing a simple sundress with an enticing row of buttons up the front in a shade of blue that emphasised her eyes, her long red hair falling in waves around her shoulders, Monica looked stunning.

'Cat got your tongue?' she quirked an amused eyebrow at him.

'You look amazing,' he told her, delighted to see her flush at the compliment. 'I see you took my advice,' he said, nodding down at the flat sandals she was wearing.

'I'm slightly concerned by your request for sensible footwear, but yes I did.' she laughed, pulling a face as she folded a matching wrap around her shoulders. 'Where are we going?'

'You'll see,' he said mysteriously, and crooked his arm for her to take. After a moment's hesitation, she slipped her arm through his and he walked her up the path and towards the gate.

'We're walking somewhere?' she asked, looking up at him, confused.

'Yup. But don't worry, it's not far.'

He carried on walking, amused by the puzzled expression on her face, and led her down the track that he used for his morning run and up the hill on the other side. As they walked through the trees to the clearing that lay beyond, she stopped dead and let out a gasp.

Glad to see that his covert arrangements with Gavin were having the desired effect on her, he waited while she took in the scene. The clearing had an unparalleled view of the valley down to the coast which was dotted with lights in this half-light. On the ground, a blanket was laid out, a picnic basket and a cooler set out for them, and the whole setting was alive with shimmering candles.

'My lady,' he said, dipping and holding out a hand, which she took, her face wonder-struck in the candlelight. When she was seated, he began to unpack the contents of the basket and laid them out, setting the plates and cutlery next to the food. Monica watched him silently, and when he uncorked the champagne, he couldn't help but say it.

'Cat got your tongue?'

She laughed then, taking the proffered flute with a nod of thanks.

'This is beautiful, Jacob. It's not at all what I was expecting.'

'That was the idea,' he said, lowering to sit beside her and holding up his champagne. 'What shall we toast to? New beginnings?'

She contemplated him, her blue eyes looking almost black in this light. 'How about to a wonderful night?'

'How about to the start of a beautiful friendship?'

'How about we just drink the damn stuff and enjoy ourselves?'

Grinning, he held up his glass and took a sip of the perfectly crisp, cold champagne, watching as she did the same.

'So, what have we got here?' she asked, looking at the containers he'd pulled out of the picnic basket.

'Ah,' he said, stretching over to reach them and pulling off the covers. 'All of madam's favourites. Coronation chicken sandwiches, sausage rolls, and salt and vinegar crisps.'

Monica gave a snort, a hand flying up to cover her face as she laughed. He joined in, he couldn't help it. That sound was music to his ears. When she'd regained her composure enough to speak, she leaned forward, plucked up a sandwich, and said to him, 'your memory is quite remarkable. I'd forgotten this myself!'

'There are some things you never forget, Mon. And your revolting habit of stuffing these sandwiches with crisps is definitely one of them.'

'See, I'd forgotten that bit too,' she grinned at him, then proceeded to wedge crisps between the bread and its overflowing filling with glee. She took a huge bite, chewing on it with relish, a satisfied smile appearing. 'Yup, it still tastes good.'

Shaking his head, he picked up a sandwich for himself, but refused to follow her lead with the crisps.

'How on earth did you organise this?'

He laughed. 'Luckily Gavin understood what was needed. I'm not sure the chef was thrilled, though. It was an offence to his French soul, apparently.'

She smirked. 'I'm not surprised. Never mind, I'm sure he'll get over it. Although pairing it with the finest French champagne must have been the final insult!'

Jacob looked at her, put his half-eaten sandwich down, and brushed a strand of her hair behind her ear. 'Nothing is too much trouble for you, Mon. It never was, and it never will be.' He saw her eyes widen and her tongue flick out to lick her lower lip, and, taking his cue, leant in to kiss her. A gentle touch to start with until she responded, and he became more urgent when her hand rose to grip his hair. As the kiss became deeper, she moaned quietly. It was the only sound in the evening air and flames of desire shattered his earlier resolve to keep things light-hearted tonight.

He leaned his whole body, pushing her slowly to the ground, shoving dishes out of the way as they lay down. Her hands were roving up and down his back hungrily, pulling at his shirt to reach his bare skin. His own hands were finding their way down her slender frame to the hem of her dress, slipping underneath and drawing gentle circles up her stomach until he reached her breasts. She let out a mewl of pleasure, her nails digging into his back as she arched towards him. Clouds of lust were swirling through his brain but he tried to reign them in, take his time and not ruin this by going too fast.

Tracing kisses down her neck, he carefully began to unbutton the dress, his lips never leaving her skin. That done, he pushed himself up, opening the fabric to reveal her body, his eyes drinking in every inch. Holding himself there, he looked up at her and saw she was watching him. Their eyes remained locked for a moment before he asked, 'are you sure, Mon?'

TWENTY - NINE

Monica's body was pulsing with desire, all rationale out the window despite her best intentions. The candlelit picnic, his thoughtfulness towards her, and his hands playing her body like a familiar tune combined with so many years without the touch of a man left her incapable of being sensible. She nodded at him, watching as his head dipped to take a nipple in his mouth, and let herself give in to pleasure completely.

'You did what?' Sam screeched down the line the next day. 'Monica Palmer, you little hussy.'

She giggled like a schoolgirl. 'I couldn't help it, Sam. It was all so... all so perfect.'

'How was he?' She could hear the grin in his voice.

'Bloody amazing, if I'm honest,' she admitted, taking a sip of coffee, eyes on the view, but images from last night playing like a cheesy movie in her head.

'Worth waiting twenty-three years for a repeat performance?'

She sobered then. As wonderful as last night had been, it only went towards complicating issues. She didn't regret it per se, but she wished wholeheartedly that the memory didn't come with a two-tonne bag of guilt.

'Yes and no,' she admitted. 'I couldn't have asked for a more perfect reunion, except for the fact that I've kept this secret from him. From them. I should have told them before I allowed things to go this far.'

Sam blew out a breath. 'It is a mighty fine pickle you've gotten yourself into, Monica. What are you going to do now?'

I've no idea, Sam. Maybe I could...' she stopped, unable to come up with a sensible answer. Jacob had said he would message her today, when they lingered for a last kiss by her door. He wanted them to go out again, and she had to admit that she wanted that too.

The whole evening had been so incredible. How could she not? After the first frantic, explosive bout of sex, they'd laid under the stars, quietly talking as they finished the food and champagne. Then they'd kissed again, slowly making love, taking their time to explore each other's bodies until the faint glow on the horizon let them know it was time to go home.

'I'm still here!' Sam's petulant voice broke into her reverie.

'Sorry, Sam. I was miles away.'

'I bet you were,' he gave a dirty chuckle. 'Listen, I have to go. I've got an appointment. For now, why don't you just focus on your art? Get some of whatever you're feeling onto canvas. Hopefully, it will inspire you with how to handle all of this.'

'Thanks, I will,' she told him and ended the call. Tabatha was still in bed, so she went back in quietly to collect her art bags. She felt sure that Jacob would actually be thrilled by the news that he had a daughter, but Tabatha? After all the half-truths she'd told her over the years when she'd asked about her dad, well, that was another story.

They had always been so close, more like sisters or friends, and this news could potentially change that forever. Monica couldn't bear that idea. But the alternative to that was keeping her secret and getting Jacob out of their life as quickly as possible, and that was an equally unpleasant thought. Now that she'd found him, she couldn't bear to let him go again. Setting up her easel, her mind awash with images from last night, she let them guide her as she started to paint.

'You've been busy,' Tabatha's voice startled her when she finally appeared. Glancing up, she saw her daughter had brought coffee and breakfast pastries out with her, and she smiled gratefully, her stomach rumbling in agreement.

'Good morning, love,' she said, putting her brush down and rubbing her face.

Tabatha set her offerings out on the table and pulled out a chair. 'You look tired. What time did you get in? I didn't hear you, so it must have been quite late,' she smirked.

Monica felt the heat rising to her cheeks and waved the question away with an airy, 'I'm not sure, I didn't check.'

Her daughter laughed. 'Well, as long as you had fun, Mum. It's good to see you relaxing for once.' She picked up a croissant and started to munch on it between sips of coffee. Monica was glad to see that she seemed to have no issue with Jacob. In fact, she seemed to genuinely like him, which was a good start. Maybe, just maybe, this fact would override any anger she might feel when the truth came out.

Her phone chimed and she swiped it open. She must have been staring at it too long as Tabatha asked, 'what's up? Is everything all right?'

'Yes, yes. It's fine,' she told her, putting it back on the table. 'It's just Jacob. He's suggesting we all go out to the beach together today.'

'Blimey, he's keen if he wants us to play happy families already,' she scoffed, standing to clear the table. 'But I'm fine with that if you are?'

'Wouldn't you rather we did something by ourselves?' Monica asked, trying to keep the hysteria out of her voice. *Happy families indeed*, she thought as she tried to think through his suggestion.

'It's cool,' Tabatha said lightly. 'I'd love to go to the beach again and it looks like you've already done enough work for today, so,' she shrugged her shoulders and carried the plates inside.

So, I really don't have any excuses, do I? She picked up her phone and stared at the message again. He was so thoughtful, trying to include the kids like this. If it was any other man, she would be delighted that they understood that she came as a package deal, but the idea of them all spending the day together was alarming to say the least.

Taking the plunge, she tapped out a quick reply telling him they would be ready in an hour. She desperately needed a shower before they went anywhere, and hopefully that would give her time to get her shit together and come up with a way to break the news to them.

THIRTY

Delighted that Monica had agreed to his plan, Jacob went to drag Nate out of bed. He knew that he was pushing things too quickly, but he was painfully aware that their time together was ticking away with each day that passed and he feared that if he let her leave without somehow cementing their relationship, Monica would disappear from his life again.

'Come on, son,' he called to the figure huddled under the covers. 'Time to get up. We're going to the beach with Mon and Tabatha.'

A startled face popped out. 'Really? That's a bit... odd, isn't it?'

'I thought you'd be pleased. A day by the sea and time with your new friend?'

'Well, yeah,' he said, sitting up. 'But it's going to be awkward.'

'Don't be daft. It'll be fine,' he replied dismissively, hoping to God he was right. 'You've got half an hour. Come on. Chop, chop!'

Nate groaned but swung his legs out, standing and heading to the bathroom. Jacob went to his room to get ready, trying to suppress the bubbles of excitement rising from his stomach. It didn't take long until they were ready and, double checking that Nate had a towel with him, they went out to find Monica and Tabatha were already there by the car, waiting.

As he drank in the sight of her, he noted again the differences between Monica and her daughter. Tabatha stood at least a head taller than her mum, her dark hair was tied back and as she gave a smile to greet them, he saw a dimple flex on her cheek. He realised he knew nothing about her father. Neither of them had mentioned him as far as he was aware, it was like he didn't exist.

'Good morning, ladies,' he called, conscious of how contrived it sounded, and coughed before continuing. 'I thought we could head to Nice, if that's ok with everyone?'

Nate gave a muted grunt, which he took for approval, and Tabatha's face lit up with a grin. 'Perfect,' she told him. 'Come on, Mum, in you get,' she said, holding open the back door of the car. Monica still hadn't said a word, but she glanced at him now before slipping into the back and sliding over to make room for Tabatha. Wondering if this had been the worst idea in history, Jacob walked around to the driver's side and got in, noticing that Nate was scowling at the seating arrangement.

As they set off in silence, Jacob struggled to find something to say.

'Well, the weather is looking good again, isn't it?'

'Quelle surprise,' Nate muttered, resolutely looking out of the side window. Tabatha gave a snort from the back and Jacob could feel his face flushing, so turned on the music to fill the silence rather than saying anything else inane.

'Aw, Dad,' Nate moaned immediately as the first notes filled the air.

'Hey, it's my turn, so my music,' he said as jovially as he could, keeping his eyes on the road.

'What's wrong with the Chili Peppers?' Tabatha queried from the back. 'I think they're fantastic.'

Jacob's eyes flicked up to the rear-view mirror to look at her in surprise. He gave her a grin. 'I'm afraid Nate doesn't share our love of 90's music.'

'More fool him,' she chuckled. 'Mum and I rarely listen to anything else, do we, Mum?'

Monica met his gaze and smiled, her face lighting up under her large sun hat. 'Some things you never forget, and music from your teenage years is definitely one of them.'

Nate sank further into his seat, a sulky expression on his face as the three of them discussed the best and worst songs from that era for the rest of the journey. When they reached La Plage d'Eze, Jacob found the parking area easily, and they bundled out of the car with their beach bags. A short flight of stairs led to the narrow strip of pebble beach that fronted the deep-blue sea. The small bay was backed by verdant hills, dotted with buildings, and the air that greeted them in the light breeze had a salty tang.

'Look, there are some free beds over there,' said Nate, finally coming out of his grump and pointing further along the beach to some turquoise beds in front of a funky-looking restaurant. The situation became awkward again when it came time to strip down to their swimwear. Monica and Tabatha seeming to hesitate as they faffed around laying out their towels and taking things from their bags. In unspoken agreement, Jacob and Nate didn't hang around and were soon diving into the wonderful warm water, giving them space to sort themselves out.

'Told you it would be weird,' Nate said when they were a little further away and out of earshot.

'Sure it is, it's something new for all of us,' he replied, slipping onto his back to float as he looked up at the clear blue sky. 'But there's only one way to get used to something, Nate. And that's by doing it.'

'Yes, oh wise one,' he scoffed and splashed a handful of water over him. Jacob sank briefly then came up with a mock roar and splashed him back, chasing him through the water. When they tired of their game, they returned to shore and found the girls settled on their sunbeds. Monica had on a fetching, emerald one-piece, but Tabatha's bikini left little to the imagination and Jacob could see that Nate was desperately trying not to stare as he took his place, book firmly in hand.

As Jacob dried himself off, he looked along the beach. 'Hey, looks like they have some water sports over there. Anyone fancy trying out a SUP board?'

Tabatha sat up quickly looking thrilled. 'Count me in!' Monica just lowered her glasses and gave a look of distaste. 'Not for me thank you, but you knock yourselves out.'

'Nate?' he asked, but the boy took one look at Tabatha as she rose to get ready and shook his head quickly. 'Looks like it's you and me, kid,' he told Tabatha and they walked up the beach together, leaving the other two staring after them with equal measure of discontent.

THIRTY-ONE

'That girl just can't sit still for a minute,' Monica said, glancing at Nate with a smile in the hope it would set him at ease. It seemed to work, as he grinned in response.

'Yeah, dad's the same. I keep telling him to chill out, but he doesn't listen.'

'I take it you don't have your dad's love of all things sport related?'

'Definitely not,' he told her, holding up his book. 'This is what I love.'

Monica wanted to ask if he took after his mother. She would love to know more about the woman who Jacob had married, but knew how hard Nate had taken her death and didn't want to upset the boy.

'Tabatha seems to love both,' she said instead. There was a moment's silence. 'I'm going to have a nap if that's ok?' she asked him. 'I was up early painting. You go ahead and read.' Relief flashed across his face as he gave a quick nod and lifted the book back up.

She closed her eyes but couldn't relax, too wired for the impending revelation, which she knew had to come soon. She cracked open one eye and scanned the water, spotting Jacob and Tabatha easily as they made their way slowly and unsteadily across the sea on the rented boards. The fact they were father and daughter was plain to see for anyone who cared to pay attention. The same build, the same stance, and the same graceful movements, even when trying something new. She let out a slow breath to even out her pulse rate, which accelerated every time she thought about the discussion ahead.

When they returned, they were laughing and joking easily, both flushed with the shared excitement of trying something new.

'Hey, you two,' Monica said. 'Looks like you enjoyed that.'

'We sure did! We're going to try windsurfing after lunch, aren't we, Tabs?' Jacob replied, picking up his towel to dry off. Monica and Nate shared a brief look of amusement before he asked, 'can lunch be soon?'

'I second that,' Tabatha agreed, plopping down on her sunbed. 'I've worked up a real appetite.'

'Well, there's a surprise,' both parents said in unison and they all burst out laughing, dispelling the last of the weirdness between them.

Ajuna Bay restaurant was a charming little place, the turquoise colour of the sunbeds repeated within as a bright contrast to the hardwood floors and high beamed ceiling. Adorned with an eclectic mix of dream catchers, driftwood designs, and rattan lighting, it had a laid-back vibe that was perfect for a chilled lunch by the sea.

As they discussed the menu, Monica could feel Jacob's gaze on her. Every time she glanced in his direction, the heat in his beautiful eyes told her exactly what he was thinking and flashbacks from last night coursed through her mind, making her squirm in her seat. Her libido was very definitely awakened from its recent hibernation, and telling her in no uncertain terms that it would like a repeat performance. He grinned at her over his menu and she pulled a face at him.

'I'm having the cheeseburger,' Nate announced, putting his menu back on the table decisively. Tabatha snorted and looked at him with disdain.

'Couldn't you try something a little more French?'

'I could, but I'm not gonna,' he smiled. 'I fancy a taste of home.'

She tutted, but with no real malice as she continued to scan the options. 'There's not much for me to choose from, but I think I'll have the asparagus salad and the minted rice,' she said finally.

'Do you want to share some oysters?' Jacob asked Monica, still with that suggestive grin on his face.

'No, I do not,' she looked up at him sharply and said primly. 'But I will share the lamb dish with you if you fancy?'

'Oh, I do fancy. I fancy it very much.'

Heat flooded her face at the undercurrent in his tone and her eyes dropped away, unable to meet that look any longer. It had been so long since she'd felt so desired, so womanly, and she realised she had missed it. She had basically given up on men and thrown herself into being a mother, her only passion creating her art, and was astonished at the revelation that this was something she craved.

Her heart pounded in her chest as she wondered wildly if she could somehow arrange to be alone with him again before the shit hit the fan. She was so frightened of losing him and Tabatha with the one short sentence that was hovering constantly on the tip of her tongue; it was paralysing.

'Are you ok, Mum?' Tabatha asked, looking at her in concern. 'You're looking a bit flushed.'

'Probably not enough sunscreen,' she told her and took a sip of water. 'I'll have to be more careful when we go back to the beach.'

Grateful when a waitress came to take their orders, Monica ordered the cheapest bottle of wine she could find. This place was quite expensive, and she wasn't sure how much longer her holiday money would last at this rate, but needed something to bolster her nerves. Only half listening to the conversation that continued around her, she felt disconnected from the situation as her mind continued to swirl in panic. Should she just blurt it out? She mentally shook away that thought. Dropping a bombshell like this needed tact, which she knew was not her strongest trait, but now was not the right moment.

Her phone pinged and she read the message, a smile lighting up her face.

'Sam's coming!' she told Tabatha who gave a whoop of delight.

'Wow, that's fabulous. I haven't seen Uncle Sam in forever. When's he coming?'

'He's actually on his way, he is at the airport right now,' Monica said happily and they began to plan animatedly what they wanted to show him whilst he was here, completely oblivious to the look of thunder on Jacob's face.

THIRTY-TWO

His heart plummeted and an icy ball of jealousy made his stomach clench at the news and the obvious delight Monica and Tabatha felt at the arrival of the mysterious Sam. The agent and the best friend, the most likely reason she had said their possible relationship would affect someone else, which he had never clarified, being so carried away with his desire for her. Was it possible that last night was just a fling and meant nothing to her? Could he be completely wrong in feeling that it had been the most perfect reunion in the history of reunions and the start of something so much bigger?

Attempting to sound normal, he asked, 'I suppose this means you two want to cut our day short?'

'If you don't mind?' Monica asked, looking at him with a slight frown.

'We can still eat first though, right?' Nate asked plaintively. Monica laughed and Tabatha replied for them. 'Of course we can, silly. He won't be here for a few hours yet.'

The food arrived and Jacob struggled to eat the lamb, which tasted like ash in his mouth, pushing it around his plate distractedly as he wondered if he should just ask her outright. But with the kids sitting there, it wasn't something he could just blurt out, so he held his tongue and tried to keep up with the conversation. When they'd had their fill, he called for the check.

'I'll get this,' he said, picking up the wallet with the receipt tucked inside.

'Absolutely not, Jacob. Let me pay for ours,' Monica insisted immediately, rummaging in her bag.

'Come on, Mon. Let me help out the artist and the student, why don't you?' he jested, but the look of anger that flared on her face told him his joke had fallen flat.

'I do not need your handouts, thank you very much. I am quite capable of looking after myself!'

He held up his hands as if to defend himself. 'Woah. I didn't mean anything by that. I was just trying to be nice.'

'Well, don't,' she replied sniffily, plucking the receipt from the wallet to check the total and counting out the appropriate amount of euros.

As they walked back to the beach to collect their things, Tabatha dropped back to walk alongside him.

'Sorry about mum,' she said quietly. 'She's very independent and gets a little crazy about things like that. Having to provide for us by herself all this time...' Brushing her hair out of her eyes, she gave a quick, apologetic shrug.

'No worries,' he threw her a smile. 'Didn't her parents help you guys out?'

Tabatha snorted. 'Not really. They basically disowned her when she insisted on having me, and it was years before they started talking again. They have what you might call a strained relationship.'

'Christ, that's a bit harsh,' he said, looking ahead to where Monica was walking with Nate. 'What about your father?' he asked tentatively.

'He was never in the picture,' she said with a shrug, seemingly unconcerned. Jacob nodded, wondering how on earth a man could leave her in that situation and not at least provide for his child. God, she must have had such a tough time of it back then. He couldn't even imagine what she had been through. No wonder she was a bit prickly now and so hesitant to open up and trust people.

On the drive back, he tried to keep the conversation light, and luckily Tabatha and Nate got into another discussion about Oxford, which filled most of the journey.

'Mon, can I have a quick word?' he asked her, as he handed her beach bag to her from the boot.

'Sure,' she said with a frown. 'Tabs, you go in. I'll be there in a minute.'

He handed Nate their bags and gestured with his head for the boy to go to the villa. 'I was hoping we could spend some more time together,' he said once the kids had left. She gazed up at him thoughtfully, and he wished he could read minds as he waited for her to reply. She let out a long breath.

'Yes, we probably should. We have things to talk about.'

Panic that those *things* might be the fact that she was already involved with someone shot through him, but he held his ground. 'So?'

She laughed. 'Let me see how long Sam is planning to stay for. After all, I can't abandon him now that he's gone to the effort of coming to see us.'

'I guess not,' he said sourly, and he saw her eyes widen in surprise, so added, 'just let me know, ok?' He lent in and gave her a kiss on the cheek, then turned and walked away before he could say or do anything stupid.

Inside, he hung out the damp towels and excused himself to go and have a shower. He was struggling to get a grip on his emotions. Last night had been so wonderful, and he'd set out this morning with great hopes for the day. Yet now he was feeling miserable and lonely and wishing he had someone he could talk to. Obviously, he couldn't burden Nate with his woes, and the thought of calling his sister about this was impossible.

He got dressed and walked out and into the kitchen to grab a beer. Nate was ensconced, as ever, on the sofa with a book, but looked up and asked, 'are we going out for dinner or eating in, Dad?'

He laughed and took a slug from the bottle before answering. 'In I guess. We can make a plan for tomorrow, maybe take the bikes out again?'

'Hmm. Maybe,' Nate said unenthusiastically. He stared at him for a moment, trying to decide his best course of action. He really didn't want to be hanging around the villa, just waiting for Monica to get in touch. 'I tell you what, I'll go and have a word with Gavin and see if he can suggest something we'd both like to do.'

'Good plan,' he grinned at him and went back to reading. Placing his beer on the side, he left to go and find Gavin, and as he walked across the courtyard, a taxi pulled up. He couldn't help but stop and eyeball the man who got out. He was as tall as him, casually but smartly dressed with a crop of tousled blonde hair, expensive sunglasses perched jauntily on his head, and even Jacob could appreciate the fact that he was incredibly good looking.

'Shit,' he muttered under his breath and hurried into the office.

THIRTY-THREE

'Sam!' Monica squealed and threw herself into his arms with relief. 'I am so glad you are here.'

'Well, there's a greeting a man could get used to,' he smiled down at her, then glanced up as Tabatha came out of her room. 'There's my favourite girl,' he said, letting go of Monica and going over to hug her. He held her out at arm's length. 'Everything ok with you, Missy?'

Tabatha gave him a quick grin and nodded. Something passed between them that Monica couldn't fathom, but they'd always been close. Sam was the closest thing to a father she'd ever had.

'I thought I was your favourite girl,' she pouted at him with an exaggerated look of dismay. He just laughed and gave her shoulder a shove.

'Oh, you know how fickle I am, Monica,' he said, walking back to the bags he'd dropped by the door and holding them aloft. 'I may have something here that will make up for it, though!'

Monica grinned. It was so wonderful to have him here. 'Have you been raiding Duty Free again, Sam Harding?'

He gave a little shimmy, causing the contents to clink. 'It's always a possibility. Lead me to the glasses.' His gaze wandered around the living area as he unpacked the bottles of champagne on the breakfast counter. 'This is really something,' he said appreciatively. 'Gavin's done an amazing job renovating this place.'

Monica looked at him curiously. 'Yes, and you still need to tell me what happened between you two.'

'I think your news is more pressing,' he said, but she saw the heat rising to his face. 'I mean, you finally getting some action. Now there's something we need to discuss.'

She scowled at him and nodded at Tabatha, who was putting the bottles in the fridge. Monica had seen the way her daughter stilled at that statement and rushed to change the subject. 'Come and look at my paintings,' she cried with more enthusiasm than was entirely warranted, although she was keen to see what he thought of her latest work. She dragged him into her room, where she had them lined up against a wall.

'I take it you haven't done the big reveal yet?' he asked from the side of his mouth. She shook her head and sighed.

'Oh, Sam. It's so difficult. I want to, I really do. But I'm terrified of what the outcome will be. I might lose them both in one fell swoop.'

She plopped down onto the bed dejectedly and watched as Sam strolled along the line of painting, taking his time to examine each one without a word. Worry bloomed in her stomach as his silence continued. What if they weren't good enough for the exhibition? Maybe this entire trip was a complete failure and, as she feared, she could no longer produce work worth showing. When he reached the end of the row, he spun around with a delighted smile lighting up his face.

'Oh my God, Monica. These are incredible!'

She sagged with relief. 'I'm glad you think so.'

'I do, I do,' he said, coming to sit next to her and wrapping an arm around her. 'I also think that with time, Tabatha will come to understand why you kept this secret.' She went to protest, but he held up a finger to silence her. 'I also think, if this Jacob, who seems to have achieved the impossible and gotten under your icy wall of independence and into your knickers, is worth anything, he will understand, too.'

'I hope you're right,' she breathed, leaning into his side, taking comfort from him.

'Of course I am. After all, I was right about this holiday being just what you needed, wasn't I? Look what you've achieved,' he waved his free hand along the row of art.

'Are we drinking this champagne or what?' Tabatha shouted from the kitchen. They looked at each other and laughed.

'She's definitely her mother's daughter, isn't she?' he asked with a raised eyebrow. 'Come on, you.' He stood, pulling her arm and leading her out to where Tabatha was waiting impatiently. Sam did the honours of expertly popping the cork, pouring out the golden liquid without spilling a drop. He handed them both a flute and held his aloft.

'Here's to being true to ourselves!'

'To being true to ourselves,' they responded, taking that first, delicious sip.

'Let's take these outside,' Tabatha said, walking out to the terrace without waiting for a response.

'Do we have an ice bucket?' Sam asked.

'Yes, in that cupboard next to the fridge. There's a bag of ice in the freezer.'

'Blimey, he's thought of everything, hasn't he?' Sam exclaimed when he opened the cupboard and looked at the contents.

'He's a very thoughtful man,' Monica said gently. 'You should go and say hi at some point.'

She saw Sam's shoulders tighten up for a beat before he pulled out the ice bucket and proceeded to fill it with ice. 'I will. But I need a couple of glasses of this before I face that particular situation.' He gave her a grin, trying to make light of it, but she could see the concern clouding his eyes.

'I'm sure he'll be thrilled to see you. But in the meantime, I'm more than happy to help you find your courage in this bottle,' she laughed, putting it into the ice-filled bucket and taking it out to where Tabatha was sitting.

As they sat and regaled Sam with news of what they had been up to so far, Monica couldn't help but wonder how Jacob was doing. He'd seemed peculiarly distressed to discover her agent was arriving, which was odd. Maybe it was just because he wanted a repeat performance of last night. As the memory of his kisses trailing down her body ran through her mind, she shivered in anticipation, despite the heat blossoming inside her. She certainly wouldn't mind abandoning herself to his caresses once more, even if it was for the last time.

THIRTY-FOUR

'I was happy to see you going out with Monica and her daughter this morning,' Gavin told Jacob as he rifled through some leaflets on his desk. 'Are you planning to go out together again tomorrow?'

'Nah,' Jacob blew out through pursed lips. 'Her agent has arrived, so I guess they'll be busy with him from now on.'

'Sam's here?' he squeaked, his eyebrows shooting up as he looked at him.

'Yeah. I take it you know the guy?'

'I did,' Gavin replied, gazing off at a point in the middle distance. 'But I haven't seen him for years.' He looked sharply back at Jacob. 'Do you know how long he's here for?'

Puzzled, Jacob stared at him and said cautiously, 'I have no idea. You'd have to ask them.'

'Of course,' he shook his head to clear it. 'Anyway, back to your original question. I gather your son would be more interested in something cultural?'

Jacob nodded, his face contorting into a grimace, and he shrugged with a *what can you do* gesture.

'Ok, well there's a tour that I can organise for you that takes in The Fondation Maeght Museum, that's a modern art exhibition. It also includes the Renoir museum, which is exactly what it sounds like, and then you explore Forteresse Medievale De Gourdon and finish up Grasse with a tour of the famous perfume factory there.'

'That sounds right up his street. How long does it take?'

'Oh, it's a full-day tour with a stop for lunch. Is that too long, were you thinking of something shorter?'

'No, that's absolutely perfect. Book us in for tomorrow, please.'

Once that was organised and he had all the details, he trudged back to the villa, deep in thought. Nate was still on the sofa. 'Aunt Genie's been calling you,' he said without looking up from his book. Jacob went to where he had left his phone charging on the counter and saw three missed calls from his sister, but nothing from Monica. He picked up his beer and took his phone outside to call her back, tossing the tour leaflet onto Nate's lap as he passed.

'That's our plan for tomorrow,' he said and left him to look through the information, fairly sure his son would love it.

'Hey, Genie,' he said when she answered.

'Where the hell have you been? I've been trying to get hold of you for a couple of days. Is everything all right?'

He winced at the concern in her voice, immediately contrite, knowing full well the fears that Caleb's sudden death had instilled in them both.

'Sorry, sis. We've just been busy having fun. I didn't mean to worry you.'

'Well, you did! So, what have you boys been doing that's so interesting you didn't have time to talk to me?'

He filled her in on their last couple of days, deliberately avoiding Monica's name and her participation in any of it. He rounded it up with a brief description of tomorrow's tour.

'Wow, that sounds great. Nate will be in his element.'

'Yeah,' he chuckled. 'I'm planning a bike ride the next day as payback!'

'Sounds fair. What about Mon? Any further interactions with her?'

He hesitated, not wanting to lie to his sister. 'Oh, she's around, you know?'

'What does that mean?' she asked sharply. He could just picture her face screwed up with worry.

'Look, we've been out, ok? Let's not make a big thing outta this.'

He heard her sigh down the line. 'I knew this would happen,' she said darkly. 'Jacob, you're a grown man, I can't tell you what to do. But please be careful, you've been through enough heartache.'

'I appreciate your concern, Genie. But it's fine. I don't think it's going anywhere, there's someone else in the picture.'

'That doesn't stop you making a fool of yourself,' she told him astutely.

Am I being foolish? He wondered as he went back inside to replenish his beer. He couldn't believe that what they had experienced the night before didn't mean anything. Not just the physical side of things, although that had been out of this world. But the closeness, the connection he'd felt as they lay there talking through the night. Surely that wasn't one-sided?

'This looks great, Dad,' Nate announced, following him into the kitchen area holding the leaflet aloft. 'What time do we get picked up?'

'9AM, son, so we'd better have an early night if I'm going to drag you out of bed in the morning.'

Nate pulled a face as he picked up the room service menu. 'Well, we'd better order dinner then.'

Jacob agreed, although the last thing he wanted to do was eat anything right now. But they ordered Boeuf Bourguignon with a side of Lyonnaise potatoes to satisfy Nate's appetite, and Jacob went to sit outside and watch the sunset while they waited. He wondered what was going on next door. He could hear their voices so they must be outside. More importantly, where was Sam going to sleep? He knew fine well that the villas all had the same configuration so there were only two bedrooms. He tortured himself for a moment with the obvious conclusion and the images that conjured up, then let out a groan of frustration. Unable to bear this feeling of helplessness any longer, he jumped and ran inside to get his phone, hastily tapping out a message to her.

Mon, I really need to see you. We need to talk.

He hesitated, trying to think if he should add anything else, but came up with nothing so hit send. This was a conversation that needed to be had face to face, not through messages where things could be misconstrued. Realising there was nothing else he could do now but wait, he left his phone on the counter and went to set the table for dinner, clinging desperately onto the hope that he had some kind of future with Monica.

THIRTY-FIVE

Next door, things were getting a little messy as they cracked open their third bottle of champagne. But they were having fun, and as usual, Sam was providing plenty of entertainment. Monica's sides were aching from laughing so much, and she thanked her lucky stars again for that fateful day when he had discovered her at a local craft fair.

Not just for the professional side of things, although if it wasn't for him, she'd probably still just be tinkering around with painting like it was a hobby rather than a career. But more importantly, for his friendship and unerring support over the years. He had become her family when she needed one and, after Tabatha, he was her favourite person in the entire world.

There was a quick succession of pings as they all received message notifications at the same time, prompting another round of ridiculous giggles.

'Oh my,' said Tabatha, wiping the tears from her eyes. 'That's Sally. I think I'll go and give her a quick call before going to bed. Uncle Sam, I've cleared all my crap off the other bed for you.'

'Thank you, sweetie. I'll try not to make too much noise,' he told her, his eyes still riveted to his screen. They bade her goodnight and Monica watched him for a minute, waiting to see if he would tell her what had made him look so serious suddenly. He finally looked up. 'It's Gavin,' he whispered in awe.

'And? What does it say?' she asked, sitting forward in anticipation.

'He says he is delighted that I'm here, and he wants to take us all to a vineyard for wine tasting tomorrow if we'd like?'

'Good man! That sounds perfect on all counts,' she paused. 'That's if you're ok with it?'

Sam nodded thoughtfully. 'I believe I am.'

'Well, there we go. That's tomorrow sorted,' Monica said, finally looking at her own message. 'Oh, God.'

'What?'

'Jacob wants to see me. He says we need to talk.'

'He's right, you do.'

She slumped back in her chair, tilted her head back, and looked up at the stars with a long breath.

'Just tell him you'll catch up with him when we get back tomorrow. I can take Tabs out if need be.' Sam looked up from his tapping on his phone. 'Don't worry, Monica, it's gonna be fine.'

'I wish I had your confidence, Sam. But thank you, having you here makes the world of difference.'

He gave a cocky grin. 'I know.'

Monica picked up a discarded cork and threw it at him. 'Alright Mr know-it-all. What time do we need to be ready tomorrow?'

'Hang on a min,' he said, fingers flying across the screen. 'Not till eleven, apparently. Good,' he said, putting his phone down and picking up the bottle. 'That means you can finally tell me all about your night with Jacob.' He waggled his eyebrows at her as he topped up their glasses.

Monica was feeling worse for wear when she woke the next morning. The champagne had left an unpleasant, sweet aftertaste in her mouth, and she stumbled into the bathroom to brush her teeth and gargle some mouthwash to get rid of it. She pulled her robe firmly around herself and went to the living area, following the sound of voices to the terrace.

'Morning, Mum,' Tabatha called cheerfully. 'Did you sleep well?'

'I guess so,' she said, pulling out a chair to join them at the table, which was strewn with breakfast fare. She looked at Sam, who was obviously fresh from a shower, already dressed and sipping happily on a coffee. 'I see you are as perky as ever.'

'No reason why not,' he smirked, despite their late night. She stuck her tongue out at him and pulled a cup towards her. 'Is there more coffee?'

Tabatha stood, poured her the last from the pot, and went to make some more.

'Are you nervous about seeing Gavin?' she asked Sam after taking her first, reviving sip.

He chuckled nervously. 'You could say that.'

'You never said what happened.'

'He decided to come here,' Sam said simply. 'He chose France over me.'

'Surely you could have worked something out?' she asked, not understanding.

He shook his head. 'There's more to it than that, but it's all water under the bridge. Let's just enjoy our day.'

She let it slide, but when they were almost ready to go, she pulled Tabatha back and called out to Sam, 'you go ahead. We'll be there in a bit.'

'What's that all about?' her daughter asked, slipping on her sandals and pulling her bag onto her shoulder.

'I just want to give them a minute.'

It seemed to have worked, as when they arrived, Sam was leaning casually against the car, deep in conversation with Gavin, who was laughing at something he'd said. They piled into his car and set off up the road, Gavin explaining they were going to see a friend of his who was an organic farmer with a smallholding where he produced his own wine, amongst other things.

Gabriel and his wife Marie were a delightful couple in their early sixties who welcomed them with open arms. Gabriel was a short, stocky man with a mop of dark hair that kept falling across his eyes while he talked animatedly about his grapes as he led them around the property. By the time they circled back to the farmhouse, Marie had set up a table under a vine-covered pergola. She smiled happily at them as they walked up and indicated they should take a seat before scurrying into the house.

There were several bottles lined up on the table containing wine of varying hues, and as they started the tasting, Marie bustled back out with plate after plate containing morsels of cheese, cured hams, olives, and salami. Wishing she'd brought her sketchbook as she looked around at the rustic scene, Monica flinched when she remembered she'd agreed to see Jacob later. Her stomach curdled in protest as she downed the first sample, but she ignored it, determined not to think about what was going to happen later.

THIRTY-SIX

To Jacob's surprise, he was actually enjoying the tour. He didn't know if it was because of Nate's enthusiasm or his growing excitement about seeing Mon later. Either way, he looked on with interest as the guide led them around the Renoir museum. The modern art gallery where they had stopped first hadn't really been his thing. But being here, where the famous artist had actually lived and worked for the last years of his life, was an entirely different experience. He and Nate gazed on in awe at the original paintings housed there, listening raptly to the guide's descriptions and backstories for each piece, bringing them to life.

The next stop was the Forteresse Medievale De Gourdon, their minibus driver expertly handling the steep, winding road that led up to the picturesque, 11th century village perched high up in the hills. They overtook several groups of cyclists on the way up and Nate turned to his dad and said with a scowl, 'don't even think about it!'

Jacob just laughed and said, 'you don't fancy the ride up here then?'

When they reached the village, their guide Babette led them through to the imposing castle, explaining how it had been built on the remains of a fortress that dated back to the 9th century and that it had been the main defence for the region. The views were unbelievable. Jacob gave up trying to capture them on his phone, the end results not doing it justice, and settled for just enjoying the moment. They were both overloaded with history and information when they exited the castle, and it delighted Nate when she told them it was now time for lunch.

Babette led them back through the village to a little restaurant called La Taverne Provençale, where the owner warmly greeted her and took them to their table right at the edge of the garden overlooking the Rue Principlae. From here, their view was unobstructed, and they could see from Nice all the way to Antibes and Cannes.

'It is impressive, oui?' Babette asked as they took their seats.

'It's outstanding,' said Jacob with an amazed shake of his head. They placed their orders, the guide letting them know the house specialties and choosing a spectacular bottle of local red wine to accompany the meal.

As they enjoyed the perfectly cooked lamb chops with an amazing grilled goat's cheese salad that even Nate ate with enthusiasm, Babette told them a little about her life, the village she had grown up in and how her love for the area had inspired her career. Her passion for her work reminded him of Monica and the way she would always light up when talking about her painting.

'What's Tabatha and her mum up to today?' he asked Nate when Babette had gone inside to use the bathroom.

Nate looked up from his phone and grinned. 'They've gone to a wine tasting thing with Gavin. Apparently, her mum and Sam are getting a bit tiddly, so Tabs is taking it easy with the wine to keep an eye on them.'

Jacob frowned at that snippet of information, wondering yet again what was going on there, and said vaguely, 'of course, Tabatha is old enough to drink. I'm glad she can be sensible with it.'

'The legal drinking age is different in England, but anyway, she'd be more than old enough whichever country you're in.'

Babette came back before Jacob could question Nate about that statement and it wasn't until they were back on the minibus and heading down the mountain towards Grasse he had the opportunity to ask him.

'So, how old is Tabatha? I thought she had just turned twenty-one.'

'Nah, she's twenty-two, Dad. In fact, it's not long until her next birthday.'

Oblivious to his father's shock at this news, Nate started to chat with Babette about the famous French writers he was so inspired by. Jacob, only dimly aware of the conversation, tried to compute what he'd just been told. If she was about to turn twenty-three, that could really only mean one thing, couldn't it? His brain scrambled to come up with another plausible explanation, but failed.

His heart was pounding as the certainty that he had a daughter settled on him like a blanket, and a huge smile broke out. He couldn't understand why Mon hadn't told him as soon as she saw him, but that didn't matter now. There were a lot of years to make up for, with both of them. He barely listened to the tour of the historic perfume factory, only registering anything when they walked into the perfumer's laboratory and the intense aromas hit them. All he wanted to do was get back to the villa and have it out with Monica. It was obvious that Tabatha didn't know who he was, so they should probably sit down with her together to break the news.

'Are you ok, Dad?' Nate queried as they walked back to the minibus. 'You've been awfully quiet.'

He slung an arm around his son's shoulder and gave him a squeeze. 'I'm fine, Nate. A bit overloaded with info, that's all.'

'I really enjoyed today. Thanks for organising this.'

'Ha! Just remember that when we go out on the bikes tomorrow,' he joked with a grin, wondering how Nate would take this discovery. The smile dropped away as he thought about Mon's agent again. He hoped against hope he was wrong about their relationship and he and Monica had half a chance of making a go of this. Especially now he knew about Tabatha.

As the bus wended its way back to the villas, he sent Monica a quick message, confirming he would be home soon and ready to meet up whenever she was free. Hopefully, he wouldn't have to wait too long to get all the answers he needed.

THIRTY-SEVEN

Tabatha was having a hard time getting Sam and her mum to leave the vineyard. It would be easier to herd a couple of cats, she thought crossly as they demanded another sample.

'Mum, you promised we would go after that last one. I'm sure Gabriel and Marie have better things to do than keep up with your demands all day.'

'Party pooper!' Sam crowed, trying unsteadily to grasp his glass again.

Gavin, who'd been watching on with amusement from the seat next to her, lent in and whispered. 'In my experience with Sam, it's better just to let him tire himself out.'

She nodded with an exaggerated sigh. 'Maybe we can bribe them. Let's buy a couple of bottles to take back.'

'Good idea,' said Gavin, standing up decisively and calling to Gabriel.

While he went inside to choose the wine, Tabatha gazed at the drunken duo affectionately. Her mum had developed hiccups and was desperately trying to hold her breath long enough to get rid of them, but Sam kept making her giggle and foiling her efforts. She had to smile. They were like kids whenever they got together. She was glad her mum was lucky enough to have such a good friend that could always make her smile, as infuriating as they could be.

They lured them to the car with the wine and poured them into the back seat while they giggled away foolishly at who knew what. Back at the villas, Gavin helped her shepherd them inside, giving Sam an extended embrace before leaving, which seemed to sober him up somewhat. He stared at the door for a while after it closed, a small smile playing around his lips.

'Look at you all love-struck,' Monica giggled as she weaved over with a freshly opened bottle.

'He's perfect,' Sam sighed with a tight smile at her as they went to sit outside.

'It would seem he thinks the same about you, Sammy boy. You should do something about that.'

'You think I should?' he asked with a hopeful look on his face.

'Definitely! You should take the bull by the horns as it were and ask him if he wants to try again.'

'You're a fine one to talk,' he giggled, looking up as Tabatha came out.

'What are you two waffling on about now?' she asked with a grin.

'Whether or not Uncle Sam should follow his heart and try again with Gavin.'

She nodded. 'Why not? If he's prepared to put up with you, then I'd say you should leap on the opportunity.'

'Oh, hilarious,' Sam growled, but couldn't keep a straight face.

'Anyway, I'm going to pop next door to catch up with Nate and see how his day was. Sounds like they did a fantastic tour today.'

'OK, just remember what I said about him,' Monica told her, taking another sip of wine.

Tabatha glared at her. 'What exactly is your issue with Nate?' she huffed. 'You seem to like Jacob well enough. Why don't you like his son?'

Monica stilled, glancing nervously at Sam, who nodded at her encouragingly.

'It's not that I don't like him, you just can't... You know, get involved with him.'

Tabatha pushed her hair off of her face in frustration. 'Not that it's any of your business who I do or don't get involved with,' she retorted. 'But why not Nate?'

Monica stared at her for a moment, then took a breath and rushed out, 'because he's your brother.'

Tabatha stood stock still, the colour draining from her face. 'What are you talking about, Mum?' The acid in her voice chilled the air between them. Monica continued to stare mutely until Sam laid a supportive hand over hers on the table.

'Jacob is your father, Tabs. I'm sorry I didn't tell you sooner. You have to understand, I thought he didn't care about us. I thought we'd never see him; I wasn't expecting all this.' She waved a hand around, knocking her glass over, and Sam leaped up to grab some napkins to sop it up, all the while watching Tabatha for her reaction.

'You told me my dad had died,' she said in bewilderment.

'Well, I never actually said that,' Monica replied sheepishly, not able to look her daughter in the eye.

'You said, and I quote, he was taken from us before I was born.'

'He was,' she muttered mulishly, still not looking directly at her.

'When I asked about where he was buried, you said his parents had taken him back to the states and wanted nothing to do with us. You implied it was a body they had taken back, not a living, breathing boy.' Tabatha's voice had risen to a screech, and she was trembling with shock and anger.

'Darling, please believe me. If I had had any idea that it was outside interference stopping him from communicating with me back then, I would have bloody swum there if I had to, just to let him know about you. But you see now why I was concerned about your friendship with Nate?'

Tabatha's face became a mask of anger. When she spoke, her voice was dripping with vitriol.

'All I see is that you have been lying to me all my life. And if you'd bothered to give Nate the time of day and had a genuine conversation with him, you would know that he's adopted. Not that it makes any difference, because if you were a little less self-absorbed, you might have noticed that I'm actually gay!' She stormed back into the villa, the slamming of her bedroom door reverberating around the building.

Monica goggled after her daughter in shock. Not because she was gay, but because it had taken this argument for her to tell her. She noticed Sam was looking off with a guilty expression on his face.

'You knew?'

He turned to her and nodded. 'Come on, Monica. It was pretty obvious. She and Sally have been an item for years.'

She clapped a hand over her mouth, blowing out between her fingers as she digested this. 'Of course,' was all she could say. 'God, what kind of mother am I that she couldn't tell me?'

Sam refilled her glass. 'That's on her, sweetie, not you. Trust me, telling your parents is the biggest thing, and it takes a while to build up to it sometimes.'

'Christ, this is all such a mess, Sam. Do you think she will ever forgive me for this?'

'Our Tabatha is a very smart girl, don't you worry. Let her sleep on it, then have a proper conversation about everything in the morning.'

'I hope you're right,' she told him as she thoughtfully took a sip of wine, her meeting with Jacob completely forgotten.

THIRTY-EIGHT

Jacob woke up and winced. He'd fallen asleep on the sofa last night waiting for Monica, and his body was decidedly unhappy about it. Unearthing his phone from where it had wedged under a cushion, he saw there were no new messages. No apology or explanation as to why she hadn't turned up last night. He sat there for a while waiting for the tumult of thoughts and feelings to settle, and was left uncertain, exasperated that nothing was resolved.

The half-light outside confirmed it was far too early to do anything about it, so he went and changed into his running shorts and set off to relieve the burgeoning tension with a workout. Pushing himself even harder than usual, he extended his run until he could barely breathe. He paused only for a moment to appreciate the glorious sunrise that was evolving before him before returning to the villa.

Once he'd showered and changed, he set about preparing breakfast for Nate's eventual surfacing, intentionally keeping busy to avoid trying to second guess what the hell was going on and what the outcome would be. Despite his annoyance with her, he desperately wanted to see Monica and hold her tightly, to let her know he was there for her now. It was possibly twenty-three years too late but, even though that wasn't his doing, he was determined to make up for it in every way he could.

The wait for Nate to wake up did nothing to dispel his anxiety. 'About time,' he growled at his son when he finally shuffled out to the terrace with a blanket wrapped around him, still looking half asleep.

'Good morning to you too,' he replied sulkily, pulling out a chair as he eyed the contents of the table. There was no further conversation until he'd finished munching on a pain au chocolat, interspersed with sips of coffee. Jacob looked on with growing agitation, unable to eat anything.

'That's odd,' Nate said, looking up from his phone, his face screwed up in concern.

'What's that?'

'It's Tabatha. She sent me a message overnight to say she was leaving.'

Jacob paused, coffee cup halfway to his mouth, his heart plummeting. 'Did she say why? Is Monica still here?' he demanded sharply.

'Nope, she didn't say why or anything else. I hope she's ok.'

'Me too,' Jacob said distantly, his brain in overdrive, trying to figure out what might have happened to cause her to leave so suddenly.

'I guess you're going to make us go out on the bikes today?' Nate asked, bringing his attention back with a jolt.

He'd completely forgotten about that threat, and going out for a bike ride was now the last thing he wanted to do. 'Nah,' he told him with a smile. 'I think we can give that a miss today. I'm just going to go next door and make sure everything is alright, then maybe we can just chill here today?'

'Cool!' Nate responded in delight, picking up another pastry, his attention back on his phone.

It was just after ten o'clock, so he figured that was a respectable time to be knocking on someone's door. Pushing back his chair, he made his way out slowly, trying to formulate his opening line. Taking a deep breath, he rapped on the hardwood door and waited.

When no sound was forthcoming after what felt like forever, he knocked again, louder this time. He heard a thud and a muffled groan before the door was finally flung open, revealing a dishevelled Sam, who looked at him blearily for a second before his face brightened with curiosity.

'Well, well, well. I assume you're the infamous Jacob?'

'I'm not sure about being infamous, but I am Jacob, yes.'

'Come on in,' he said, standing back. 'You and I need to talk, and I require coffee for this particular task.'

Jacob gave a curt nod and walked in, casting around for any sign of Monica, but she wasn't there. He watched the man with distrust for a while as he prepared his coffee before impatience kicked in.

'I really wanted to talk to Mon. Where is she?'

'Well, Romeo, she's not here, so you'll just have to make do with me,' Sam replied with an impish grin and a waggle of his eyebrows.

'No offence, but you're the last person I want to talk to,' Jacob snapped, glowering at him.

Sam feigned mock horror. 'Why ever not? I'm fabulous!'

'Tell me, what exactly is your relationship with Monica? I mean, I know you're her agent, but...' he trailed off, unable to verbalise his fear.

A flash of surprise shot across Sam's face before he gave a howl of laughter. 'Oh, my,' he muttered between giggles. 'I can assure you, your jealousy is completely misplaced. I'd be more likely to have a fling with you, if you know what I mean?'

Heat rose to Jacob's face as the implication made itself known, but relief washed through him. At least that was one question answered. He gave a crooked grin.

'Ah, I see. But what about Monica? Where is she?'

'I'm afraid she's had to leave. There was a bit of an altercation last night between her and Tabatha. When we got up this morning, Tabatha was gone and Monica has followed her. She got Gavin to take her to the airport a while ago.'

Jacob stared at him in confusion, anger slowly burning to the surface. There was so much they needed to talk about, and it wasn't exactly a conversation that could be put on the back-burner.

'How could she just leave like that, without a word?'

'To be honest, it was a knee-jerk reaction. I'm not sure that Monica had anything else on her mind other than making things right with her daughter. I wouldn't take it personally.'

'What was it about? The argument. Was it about me?'

Sam gave him a long, cool look. 'You know, don't you?'

Jacob gave a tiny nod. 'She's mine, isn't she?' he whispered.

THIRTY-NINE

Unbelievable fear shot through Monica when she had discovered Tabatha's bed empty, early the next morning. The outcome she'd most dreaded from revealing to Tabs that she had a father, apparently coming to fruition. Her note had simply said that she needed time to think and gave no further information as to where she had gone or how long for.

With tears threatening to overcome her, she urgently shook Sam awake.

'She's gone, Sam. Tabatha's gone,' she wailed before his eyes even had time to focus. Gathering his wits about him quickly, he took the proffered note from Monica's hand and scanned it. Rubbing his eyes, he said, 'hmm. That's not much help, is it?'

'Her phone is off. I have to find her. I need to explain everything properly to her.'

'Ok, ok. Take it easy, let's think this through sensibly,' he said with an encouraging smile as he flung back his covers and stood up. 'As far as I'm aware, she doesn't know anyone here in France?' he asked as he shrugged on his robe and led them into the living room.

'I don't think so,' Monica replied, a fierce look of concentration on her face.

'So, let's assume she's headed back to England. At a guess, I'd say she's on a plane now as her phone is off.'

'But how would she get... Uber!' Monica grabbed her phone and frantically started swiping. 'Yes, she booked a car with our account a few hours ago to get to the airport.' She flopped onto the sofa with relief that she had some idea where Tabatha was.

'Aha,' Sam said as he paced the room. 'So, we have the means, we just need to work out the where.'

Monica looked at him affectionately and laughed. 'Settle down, Sherlock. I would imagine she's gone home.'

'That's where you're wrong, my dear Watson,' he stopped pacing and held up a finger dramatically. 'As you would know, if you had ever had a genuine relationship, the first thing she'd do is run to Sally's arms for comfort.'

As it turned out, they were both wrong, which Monica discovered when her mum called not long after she had landed back in England. Sam had been a complete diamond and paid for the last ridiculously expensive seat in business class for her, and then gone over to wake Gavin up to give her a ride to the airport. All she'd had to do was throw a few things in her carry-on, leaving him to deal with the rest.

'Hi, Mum. I don't really have time to talk right now,' she said breathlessly as she raced through the crowds to catch the train.

'I thought you'd want to know that a rather distressed Tabatha has just turned up,' her mother told her, stopping her in her tracks. Monica stood, being buffeted by annoyed commuters as she calculated the journey to Wales. The train would take far too long. She would have to go home and get her car.

'I'll be there as soon as I can,' she muttered, and closed the call without wasting time on questions or the accusations that rose like bile. There would be enough time for all that later once she was face to face with them.

When she reached her flat, she didn't pause to change, just grabbing her car keys and a couple of bottles of water for the journey before jogging up the road to her car. It was only as she was crawling along, snagged in the rush-hour traffic, that her thoughts fluttered to Jacob and guilt flushed through her. She should have messaged him, told him something, anything. Even if it was just that there was no hope for the two of them.

Monica realised now that she had been living in a dream world to think they could just pick up where they'd left off. There was no way she could stomach losing him again as she inevitably would. Tabatha's disappearance reminded her how tenuous relationships could be, no matter how deep the bond, and how painful things could be when they ended. Cranking up the radio to drown out her morbid thoughts, Monica drove like a woman possessed, only stopping once at the services after she'd crossed the Severn Bridge for a necessary toilet break and some petrol.

Barely noticing the dramatic scenery as the car drove down through the sweeping mountains towards Aberystwyth, she focused on the GPS instructions to remind her of the route to her parents' place, trying to remember the last time she had visited them. Ever since Tabs had been old enough to get herself there if she wanted to visit, Monica hadn't felt so obligated to go. And with a start, she realised it had probably been at least five years since she'd last seen them. *I am not going to feel guilty about that; she* thought angrily, shoving away any feelings of remorse as she looked for the last turn. Spotting it just in time, she indicated and swung in, slowing to a crawl and hoping her suspension would survive the unmade lane that led to their house.

The pretty, whitewashed cottage soon came into view, creating butterflies in her stomach as she tensed in apprehension for the scene to come. She got out of the car slowly, distracted by the garden's disrepair. The usually pristine pathway was punctuated with weeds, her mother's prize rose beds wild and unkept, and the lawn was high enough to keep a goat happy for at least a day.

Before she had time to process this, the front door was flung open and Tabatha bombed out, flinging her arms around her with a sob.

'I'm so sorry, Mum,' she snuffled into her neck. 'Grandma told me everything, not letting you know that Jacob wanted to see you again, about the letters that they hid.' She stood upright and looked down at her with a watery grin. 'I wish you hadn't lied to me, but I kinda get it now,' she sniffed.

Oh, thank God, Tabs. I was terrified that I was going to lose you.' She reached in and hugged her again, relishing the feel of her. 'Right,' she said firmly after a moment. 'Let's go inside. There are things I need to say to my parents.'

FORTY

After a couple of hours talking with Sam, Jacob had to admit that he liked the guy. Now he was no longer a threat, he could relax as they drank copious amounts of coffee while Sam filled him in on the events of last night with a dramatic flair that seemed to be his norm.

'So that's why she hasn't told me, because she was scared of Tabatha's reaction?'

'Uh huh,' Sam grinned at him. 'That and yours, she was enjoying getting to know you again, if you know what I mean,' he said with a lascivious wink that had Jacob blushing beetroot red once again.

Despite this new knowledge, he just felt disappointment and anger towards Monica. He had truly believed that they had a unique connection and understanding, but the fact that she didn't trust him to stick around was proof that this was just his flight of fancy. As painful as it was, he would have to let go of any hopes of a relationship with Mon and just concentrate on developing one with his daughter. Although that meant he would still have to talk to her if he was going to be in Tabatha's life as he fully intended.

'Anyway,' Sam continued, oblivious to his inner turmoil. 'I've decided to stick around for a few days. I have some unfinished business of my own to deal with, but if you need any help with anything, you'll know where to find me.'

'Thanks, bud,' he said, standing to leave. 'But to be honest, I'm not sure how much longer I'll be here,' he told him as a plan started to form.

Back at the villa, Nate was lying on a sunbed looking for all the world like he had fallen back asleep. Jacob scooped up some pool water and splashed it over him.

'Oi!' he yelped and jumped up. 'What was that for?'

'Just checking you're still awake,' he chuckled. 'Listen, Nate. I was thinking maybe we should head to Oxford early? I'd love the chance to look around the place and get you settled in.'

Nate beamed at him. 'Really, Dad? That would be amazing. Truth be told, I'm a little nervous about being there by myself, so having you around for a few days would help ease me in, you know?'

'Great. Let me check out flights and stuff and we can get organised.'

Heading back inside to find his iPad, Jacob let out a sigh of relief that Nate was on board with the new plan. There was no way he could sit around here doing nothing, it just wasn't in his nature. And until either Monica responded to one of the messages he'd sent her, or Tabatha reached out to him on her own, he needed to keep active and feel in control. And at least this way he'd be in the right country if Tabs wanted to meet up.

It didn't take long for him to find flights and work out the train route to Oxford, and he found a beautiful old hotel called The Randolph that was within walking distance from the station and the university. He then focused on tidying up things this end, letting Gavin know they were leaving early and arranging for the bikes and the moped to be picked up. Finally, he called the rental company to say he would be bringing the car back to the airport tomorrow.

He stared out of the window thoughtfully, running through everything in his mind to make sure he'd checked all the boxes. With a satisfied nod, he went back out to the terrace.

'It's all organised, Nate,' he called. 'We leave tomorrow morning. Shall we go up to the village one last time and splurge on an extravagant lunch?'

As expected, Nate was delighted with the idea and ran inside to get dressed. While he waited, Jacob tried to call Monica, but the call went straight to voicemail. He let out a frustrated sigh. Damn that woman, why did she have to be so difficult? He thought again about that magical night they'd spent together and his heart felt like it would burst open with pain, knowing it would never happen again.

'I'm ready, Dad,' Nate shouted and Jacob gathered his thoughts before going inside. As he drove them up to St Paul de Vence for the final time, he thought about Sarah and how much she had loved it here. Aware that he hadn't really thought about her for a couple of days made him feel sad. He knew it was all part of the healing process with grief, but the fact that it had been another woman that had been taking up headspace left him full of remorse. Especially as that woman was now ignoring him. It was like being abandoned by Monica all over again, but unlike when he was seventeen, now it was just making him angry.

It was already busy in the village, and it took him a while to find a parking spot. As they wandered through the cobbled streets looking for a restaurant with an available table, he remembered that he needed to buy some wine and cheese for Genie and her husband. He and Nate took great amusement from buying the smelliest cheeses they could find in the delicatessen, knowing it would drive Genie insane as she hated the stuff.

'Hopefully she won't be too pissed at us,' Nate laughed as they came out of the shop. 'Have you told her about our change of plans?'

'Not yet. I'll message her later,' he told him, looking at the empty screen on his phone for the millionth time. He would have to tell his sister the news that she was an aunt yet again, and he really wanted to sit Nate down and explain it to the boy while they were still together. They had always been honest with Nate about where he came from and made sure he knew he was special, that they had chosen him, and Jacob wanted to make sure he understood that this was still true, even though he now had a biological daughter.

But before any of that could happen, he needed to talk to Monica.

FORTY-ONE

Her parents had aged quite shockingly in the years she'd been absent. Her mother, who stood next to the chair where her father sat by the fire, was nervously wringing her hands. The remarkable head of hair that Monica had inherited from her was now a faded, dirty blonde colour, and no longer the fiery red. A hand fluttered up nervously to pat it, as if she could feel her daughter's assessment.

Her father looked wizened, hunched up in his seat. The blanket over his lap added to the air of frailty as he looked at her, but his eyes were still bright with intelligence.

'Mum, Dad,' she said, her arm still firmly clasping Tabatha. She thought about all the things she wanted to say to them. How angry she had been that they had obliterated her chance of happiness with Jacob. But looking at them now, words failed her.

'Hello, sweet pea,' her father said, and letting go of Tabs, she strode over, bending down to give him a heartfelt hug. As she stood up, her mother reached out and patted her arm. 'Tea?' she enquired mildly, her universal panacea for everything and anything. Monica followed her into the kitchen, leaving Tabatha to keep her grandfather company, and watched as her mother went through the familiar motions to prepare an enormous pot of tea. As she waited for the kettle to boil on the gas hob, she took out a plate, added a doily and carefully arranged biscuits from a large tin on it. Then she stretched up, and pulled out another tin from the cupboard above the hob, and held it clasped to her chest protectively before at long last looking directly at Monica.

'You know, as parents, we can only do what we think is best for our children in any given situation. Even if what we do turns out to be wrong.' She gave a hopeful smile and held out the tin to her.

'What's this?' she asked, taking the rusted container in confusion, turning it over to reveal its meaning. The faded gold lettering declared it contained traditional English tea, not anything relevant to the conversation.

'The letters. His and yours. Despite everything, I didn't feel I had the right to destroy them.'

'That's rich, after what you did!'

She glared at her mother for a moment, then sagged. After all, what was the point now? Putting the tin on the counter, she carefully wiggled the top until it reluctantly popped open, scattering rust particles across the surface. Almost reverently, she lifted out the faded, unopened envelopes, recognising her own childhood scrawl and Jacob's more sturdy lettering. She traced the return to sender stamp on her own letters with her finger, lost in thought.

What a waste. All those years, they could have been happy together. Tabatha could have known her father, he could have held her in his arms as a baby, taught her how to ride her first bike, and all the other things that dads did for their daughters. Their life could have been so different. She stowed the letters gently back in the tin and placed the lid carefully back on, firmly clicking it into place. She would deal with them another time, when she was feeling a little less exhausted and wrung out with emotions. There had been enough to cope with for one day.

Later that evening, after her parents had gone to bed, she sat curled on the sofa with Tabatha and told her all about her father. How he had made her feel back then, that he was the most thoughtful person she had ever known and was always up for an adventure with her, whatever hairbrained scheme she came up with. Grinning as she recalled some of the scrapes they had got into, she looked at Tabs and said, 'you're very like him.'

'I'm quite happy with the bits that are just like you, Mum.' Her eyes dropped for a moment. 'Do you think he'll like me?'

'Of course he will. What's not to like? You're smart, funny, and beautiful... that bit you get from me.' They both laughed for a moment before Monica continued, 'Sam tells me Jacob's worked out that you're his. So, now it's up to you what to do next. I'll support you whatever you decide.'

Tabatha tugged nervously on a strand of hair as she thought about it. 'What about you? Have you been in touch with him?'

'Oh, I think we've had our chances, Tabs. It's better if we both move on.'

'Well, that's just sad. Any fool could see he is really into you, and the way you smile when he's around? I've never seen that before.'

'That's as maybe,' she said with a dismissive shrug, although her insides twisted with grief. 'Anyway. You and Sally?'

Tabatha flushed, her face becoming serious as she blew out a long breath. 'I am so sorry I didn't tell you sooner. It just never felt like the right time, there was always some drama going on.'

'I can hardly scold you for keeping secrets,' she grimaced.

'I guess not.' Tabatha held up her mug, 'here's to no more secrets?'

'God, yes,' she replied emphatically. 'I'm not sure I could cope with any more.'

As she tried to get comfy in the lumpy single bed in the attic conversion, Monica's thoughts drifted back to France, and not just because of the luxurious king-size she'd left behind. She couldn't help but wonder how Jacob was dealing with the news that he suddenly had a daughter. The messages he'd sent her throughout the day just demanded that they needed to talk and hadn't expanded on that.

Flipping over, trying to find a part of the mattress that didn't have springs poking up, she sighed. It would have been nice if he'd said something about them, but she guessed he'd reached the same conclusion, that their chance of love was long gone. When she finally replied, she'd just told him that Tabatha now knew everything and would be in touch when she was ready.

Fighting back the tears and giving up on trying to sleep, she flicked the bedside light back on and rummaged in her bag for her Kindle. *I may not get my happy ever after*, she thought, *but at least I can read about it.*

FORTY-TWO

The chill in the English air came as a shock after weeks of warmth in the French Riviera. Glad he had a coat with him, Jacob tugged it around his body and zipped it as they stood next to their cases on the platform at Oxford, trying to get their bearings.

'I think it's this way, Dad,' Nate told him, looking up from his phone, giving a thrust of his chin to point the way.

'Lead on, Macduff,' he said, trying to sound cheerful. He had hoped so much for something more from Mon when she had replied to his messages. His heart leapt when he saw her name flash up on his screen. But the message had been simple and almost cold, as if they were strangers who just happened to have a daughter, not long-lost lovers with a second chance of a future. And try as he might, it was hard to shift the melancholy that settled on him.

'Look at you trying to quote Shakespeare,' he said with a grin. 'I think I might be rubbing off on you.'

As they entered the opulent lobby of the hotel, Nate spun in circles, mouth open, head craned, trying to take in all the details. The gothic-inspired building was classic Victorian, the dark hardwood floors and elegant, ornate light fittings lending a theatrical air. 'Wow,' was all he could say over and over while Jacob checked them in.

They spent the next couple of days exploring the historic city, starting with the university where Nate would be spending his weeks immersed in his beloved literature. The on-site visit set Jacob's mind at rest to some degree. The accommodation provided was more than adequate, and the only entrance was manned twenty-four hours a day, so he felt he would be safe there. And although Nate was more intent on investigating the libraries, there were a host of activities included in the curriculum, which meant he would still get some exercise and hopefully make some friends. They joined a walking tour that was skewed more towards where various Harry Potter scenes had been filmed, and took the obligatory river cruise down the Thames from Folly Bridge towards Iffley Lock.

With its academic atmosphere, its historical and cultural richness, and a vibrant social scene, Oxford seemed to bring out the best in Nate, and as much as he was going to miss his son when he returned home, he knew it was the perfect place for him to experience his first taste of independence. It was on the morning of the third day that Jacob received a message from Tabatha asking if they could meet. She knew from Nate that they were in Oxford, and had apparently travelled up to stay with a friend in the hopes that they could meet.

His stomach lurched with nerves and excitement and he quickly devised a plan where Nate could spend a couple of hours at The Bodleian Library, which he'd been itching to do since they'd arrived.

'Are you sure it's ok, Dad?' he asked, making Jacob feel guilty for the subterfuge, but hopefully after this meeting he could tell Nate everything.

'Yes, of course, it's fine. I'm going to go for a coffee at The Grand Cafe and relax for a while,' he replied, happy with this half-truth.

The quaint cafe was the epitome of English Victorian, which made him feel out of place and added to his nerves as he secured a table in the corner to wait for her. His fingers beat an idle tattoo on the small, wooden table, only stilling when Tabatha walked in. She spotted him easily and weaved her way through the crowded cafe. As she stopped beside the table, they both hesitated, unsure how to greet each other now.

She swept her hair off of her face and grimaced. 'Well, this is awkward,' she mugged, pulling out the chair opposite him to sit, her face curious and her gaze direct.

'You could say that,' he joked feebly, his eyes raking her features for similarities. She grinned, and a dimple appeared. God, how hadn't he spotted it before? Everything from her dark unruly hair, the unusual colour of her eyes, and the smile that was the spit of his own screamed his input to her DNA.

'Let's start again,' he said, reaching a hand across the table. 'Hi, I'm Jacob Riley, and I'm your dad.'

They spent the next two hours getting to know each other a little, soon building a tentative rapport as their similarities became apparent. The conversation was lousy with exclamations of 'me too!', and she laughed after the last one, telling him, 'this feels like a first date.'

'A good one, I hope?'

'I think so,' she smiled at him. 'What are you going to say to Nate?'

He blew out a breath as he considered this. 'The truth?' he shrugged, and she nodded in agreement, then looked down at her cup, spinning it restlessly in a move reminiscent of her mother.

'What about Mum?' she asked quietly. 'She's miserable, you know? Even with her big show coming up next week. I know it's because of you.'

He considered her for a moment, trying to quell the surge of hopeful excitement that was threatening to overcome him.

'She's made it pretty clear that it's over. Her silence speaks volumes, Tabatha,' he told her, watching her face intently.

'Gah! You two are ridiculous. You're not still teenagers. There's nothing stopping either one of you from reaching out now except pig-headedness.'

She picked up her vibrantly coloured bag from the floor and rifled through it, pulling out a leaflet and sliding it across the table. 'Here are the details of her show. You might want to develop an interest in art next week.'

Jacob stared down at the slip of paper, taking in the details. Should he go and try and see Monica, or was he just opening himself up to more heartache? With his heart pounding and his blood thundering in his ears, he looked up at his daughter and gave a tiny nod.

FORTY-THREE

'Monica, snap out of it,' Sam demanded petulantly. 'I know your heart is broken, blah, blah, blah, but today is important.'

'That's easy for you to say now that you're all loved up with Gavin again!'

'I know, honey,' he said in a kinder tone and came to sit next to her. They were in Monica's flat, choosing her outfit for the show later on. 'And I've tried not to flaunt it in your face, but it's tricky. What with him being so yummy and everything.'

She turned and gave him a genuine smile. 'I'm happy for you, Sam. I really am. You make the perfect couple.'

'We do, don't we?' he preened. 'Anyway, I think you should go for the blue dress. It suits you perfectly and makes you look fabulous, even if you don't feel it.'

When he left, she cleared away the discarded outfits, slotting them back into the wardrobe in her bedroom. Walking back into the lounge, she glanced again at the mantelpiece where the tin containing the letters had sat since she'd got back, like an urn containing the ashes of their relationship. She considered it for a moment, debating. Making a decision, she stalked to the fridge, pulled out a bottle of chardonnay, and poured a hefty glass before picking up the tin and putting it on the coffee table. Taking a swift gulp of wine, she then pried off the lid and took out Jacob's letters, sorting them into date order.

Taking her time, she opened each one and read it in its entirety before starting the next. The plaintive tone that increased with each note teared at her heart, but she battled on despite the tears coursing down her face. The final paragraph of the last letter was her undoing, and it dropped from her hand, fluttering to the floor unheeded as she sprawled on the sofa, sobbing her heart out. When the tears dried up, she pulled herself upright, wiping her eyes with her sleeve, and sniffed.

'Get a grip, Monica,' she told herself sternly, and drained the rest of her glass. But the words continued to dance before her eyes as she showered and got ready for her show. They persisted as she carefully applied her makeup, and they followed her as she went down to the street to get in the car that Sam had arranged to take her to the Tate. The streets of London slid by like an art-house film in her dreamlike state, and it was only when they drew up outside the former Bankside Power Station that she surfaced sufficiently to thank the driver and make her way inside.

There was muted chatter in the room that was housing her exhibition, and Sam bounded over as she entered with a look of delight on his face. 'Looks like we're going to have a full house,' he said gleefully. Then, taking in her countenance, asked, 'are you ok?'

She smiled bravely. 'I'm fine, Sam. Just get me some of that damn champagne that we've forked out for and I'll be even better.'

He deftly swiped a couple of glasses from the tray of a passing server and, courage in hand, she followed him to do the rounds of meet-and-greets that were essential for these shows. As she chatted with the various reporters and potential buyers, she surreptitiously eyed her work, delighted to see that a few already sported the red dots that indicated a sale.

'Mum, you look amazing,' Tabatha said, arriving with her usual whirlwind speed and pulling her into a hug.

'Thank you, darling,' she laughed once she'd extricated herself from the embrace. As her daughter stood back, she noticed Sally hovering off to one side. It was the first time she'd seen them together since the big revelation. 'Sally, how lovely of you to come,' she said warmly, walking over and kissing both of her cheeks in welcome.

'My pleasure, Miss Palmer. I have to say, what I've seen so far is amazing. You've really outdone yourself.'

'Thank you, and I think you can call me Monica now, don't you?'

Ignoring the underlying sorrow that weighed her heart, Monica kept the smile on her face and the conversations light-hearted. This show could make or break her career, and after years of struggling, she was determined to give her all to this opportunity. When Sam's voice sounded through a sound system, she looked up in shock and listened in disbelief as he thanked everyone for coming and started what was obviously an introduction to the artist. *What the hell was he thinking? They hadn't discussed her speaking like this!*

She hastily swapped her empty glass for a full one as her mind scrambled for a speech that needed to endear her to the people in this room. The resounding applause gave her cue, and she walked to where Sam was waiting, holding out the microphone, an innocent look on his face.

'I'm going to kill you for this,' she hissed at him before bringing the microphone to her mouth. There was a squeal of feedback and she held it further away, eyes focused on Tabatha, who was giving her a double thumbs up in support.

'Thank you all for being here today,' she started, floundering for the next sentence. 'I would also like to give huge gratitude to my amazing agent, Sam Harding, for all the work that has gone into this exhibition.' There was a smattering of applause, and Sam bowed deeply in appreciation, giving her a wink on the way down. Heat rose to her face as she tried to think of something to say.

'I... I guess that's it really, unless anyone has any questions?' she asked hopefully, relieved when a bevy of hands shot up. Before she could select someone, a deep familiar voice piped up from the back of the room.

'I have a question for you, *Monica* Palmer.' The inflection on her name confirmed what she already knew, and her eyes darted to where the man stood towering at the back of the crowd, her eyes locking with Jacob's. He gave her that grin that made the dimple appear, and as her body responded in delight, he continued.

'I'd like to know what inspired your current collection?'

FORTY-FOUR

Jacob waited with bated breath for her to answer and kept his gaze firmly on hers, allowing her no room to escape this time. The source of her inspiration had been immediately apparent to him as he'd briefly walked around the exhibition. He saw the fire of defiance light up her eyes and the determined shift of her features as she set her jaw to meet his challenge, and the hope that had been simmering flared through him.

'Well, sir,' she said in a low voice that set his pulse racing. 'As many of you have mentioned, these paintings are quite a contrast to my usual work.'

'Why is that, do you think?' he demanded quickly. He saw her cast her eyes over the expectant crowd before meeting his gaze again and saying clearly, 'I think it's because something inside me changed, allowing me to paint from the heart.'

'And what was it that changed?'

'I did. I opened up my heart to possibility. Love inspired these paintings.'

As the crowd peppered her with further questions, he watched on with what he was sure was a ridiculous grin on his face. Sam finally stepped in and called a halt to it, inviting everyone to enjoy the champagne and canapes provided. Jacob didn't move, letting her come to him through the crowd, her eyes constantly seeking him out as well-wishers waylaid her. When she finally stood in front of him, she put her hands on her hips and looked at him with a scowl.

'Well played, Jacob Riley. Well played.'

'I had to do something to get you to admit that you love me. God knows we've wasted enough time.'

'That is true,' she whispered and stepped forward. He wrapped his arms around her and lowered his mouth to meet hers, claiming his love for her with one gentle kiss. The crowd faded away, and in this moment, there was just the two of them and the unstoppable connection that had always been between them.

'Get a room, you two,' Sam quipped, and they jumped apart slightly breathless, grinning sheepishly at him. 'Monica, despite all this,' he waved a hand to encompass them both. 'You still have a room to work. Get out there, girl!'

Jacob stood back impatiently as she complied, unable to take his eyes off her. Monica looked absolutely radiant as she talked with collectors and reporters alike, no doubt charming them with her wit and humour. The flurry of red stickers that were adorning her paintings as she made her way around the room confirmed that the evening was a triumph.

As the crowd began to thin, Tabatha and Sally stopped by to say goodnight. 'We're making a move now,' she told him. 'Tell Mum I said well done and I'll catch up with her tomorrow.'

'You could wait and tell her yourself,' he suggested.

'Nah, I'm going to give you guys some space tonight.' She gave him a cheeky grin and a wink as they walked out the door, leaving him flushed with embarrassment. *Should a daughter imply things like that?* This was all still too new for him to know what to expect.

Sam interrupted his thoughts, appearing with yet another glass of champagne for him and Gavin, who pumped his hand enthusiastically, firmly by his side.

'Great to see you, Jacob. I'm glad your visit to my villas has had such serendipitous results,' he beamed.

'For all of us, it would seem,' he said, raising his eyebrows at the happy couple. They obviously had no such worries about embarrassment and hugged each other close.

'Well, it was all my idea for Monica to go on holiday. You should be thanking *me*, really,' Sam claimed, but with no real weight to the statement as he gazed lovingly at Gavin.

'Remind me to buy you a beer sometime,' Jacob said, laughing at the agent's face of distaste at the idea as they watched Monica walk towards them. 'Make it champagne and you've got a date,' he told him before sweeping Monica up and twirling her around.

'Well done, missy,' Sam told her. 'I think we can safely say you are a success.'

'That's in no small part thanks to you, Sam,' she giggled as he set her back down.

'Oh, pish, posh. Accept a compliment for once, Monica!'

As they said their goodbyes, Monica and Jacob could barely keep their eyes off of each other, but it wasn't until they were ensconced in the privacy of the car that they spoke.

'Hello, you,' he murmured, leaning in to trace kisses across her face.

'Jacob, the driver,' she said primly, leaning away slightly. Ignoring her protest, he pulled her back and said, 'Frankly, my dear, I don't give a damn. You should be kissed, and often, by someone who knows how,' before kissing her deeply. Her laughter interrupted his passion.

'Two Gone with the Wind quotes. Bravo.'

'I've got over twenty years of making up to do,' he grinned, 'in all the ways.'

She shivered in anticipation, the air between them thick with desire.

'I read your letters. Did you mean what you said in the final one?'

He cocked his head, his eyes sparkling, a gentle smile on his lips. 'Do you mean, *time and distance have no impact, I will love you all through this lifetime, and the next, and the one after that if needs be, until we are together again*?'

She sighed, 'yes, that's the one.'

'Every damn word,' he said, reclaiming her lips with his. And this time she didn't protest.

EPILOGUE

Monica woke with a smile on her face, as she so often did these days. The gentle snoring next to her let her know Jacob was still sound asleep, so she got out of bed carefully, trying not to disturb him. Creeping out to the kitchen, she prepared some coffee and went out to the terrace to admire the sunrise. They were back in France to celebrate her birthday, which, surprisingly, didn't bother her as much as she'd expected. She had so much to be grateful for now. Being in her forties was no longer an issue when she had so much to look forward to.

As she sipped her coffee, she reflected on how much her life had changed in the last year. Her career had taken off after that show at the Tate, and she continued to paint from her heart, inspired every day by the man who adored her so blatantly and fiercely that she couldn't doubt him for a second. There had been many transatlantic flights in the last twelve months, so they could spend as much time together as possible while they worked out how their life together would look.

A knock at the door startled her, and she opened it with a puzzled expression that transformed into one of joy when she saw that Tabatha and Nate were standing there grinning at her.

'Happy birthday, Mum,' Tabatha yelled, grabbing her and pulling her off of her feet in an enthusiastic embrace.

'Surprise,' Nate said with a self-conscious shrug of his shoulders.

'Come here, you,' Monica told him, pulling him into a group hug. 'I can't believe you're both here. I thought you were too busy.'

'It wouldn't be much of a surprise if you knew,' Jacob's voice came from behind her, and she spun around to kiss him.

'Best birthday presents ever,' she told him breathlessly. 'Come on in, you two.'

'Hold up,' Gavin called as he came down the path towards them, pushing one of his delivery trolleys, embellished with multicoloured balloons. 'Breakfast for the birthday girl,' he announced as he drew up.

They made their way inside, chattering happily as they prepared the table for breakfast, and when it was set, Jacob popped open the bottle of champagne and poured them all a glass.

'To the birthday girl,' he toasted, taking a sip, before placing the glass on the table and walking over to stand in front of her. 'Mon, you are the light of my life and I don't want to spend another day without you.' He dropped to one knee, taking a small velvet box from the pocket of his robe and opening it to reveal its twinkling contents. 'Would you do me the ultimate honour and agree to become my wife?'

She looked down at him in shock, aware the kids were avidly staring at her, waiting for her reply. They didn't have to wait long, as the answer bubbled up and burst out of her with no thought required.

'Yes, Jacob. Yes, I will!' Tears of joy were running down her face and he stood, wiping them away with a finger before taking her hand and sliding the ring on.

THE END

I hope you enjoyed this romantic escape to France. If you'd like to know what happens next with Monica and

Jacob, you can sign up for my newsletter and get a bonus scene here[1].

Alternatively, you can find all my books and follow me on Amazon.

<u>US</u>[2]

<u>UK</u>[3]

You can also find me on all social media, but I share most of my goings on in my Facebook[4] page so follow me there for updates, Greek life and the occasional picture of my animals!

---

1. https://storyoriginapp.com/giveaways/9be16fc6-9892-11ed-af08-b3295b1d1742

2. https://www.amazon.com/stores/Joy-Skye/author/B08S386CV1

3. https://www.amazon.co.uk/Joy-Skye/e/B08S386CV1

4. https://www.facebook.com/JoySkyeAuthor